TABLE OF CONTENTS

NO JUSTICE
NO PEACE
BLM

INTRO:

How Did We Get Here?

"However long the night,
the dawn will break."

African Proverb

THE JUSTICE COLLECTIVE
NO JUSTICE
NO PEACE
BLM
The ultimate Student News
Source to combat the fake
reality of our racist society.

Dear twin brother, it's been less than two weeks since you were taken from us. But it seems so much longer, I truly have no idea how I can ever survive without your presence.

Ever since we were born, you were my rock even though we were two entirely different peas that harvested from the same motherly pod and hatched at nearly the same exact time.

And even though you're no longer here to receive your degree in person, no one can deny the positive impact you've had on Deacon Valley High.

As today will forever be known in history as OUR graduation day!

XO XO, Shaniece 'lil sis' Davis

NO JUSTICE
NO PEACE
BLM

CHAPTER 1:

To Mind Your Own Business.

Subject: Deshawn Davis

"Slavery is not African History. Slavery interrupted African History."

Mutabaruka

1.1 A JOURNEY TO DEACON VALLEY

I was born & raised in New Orleans, to a mother and father who were the notorious king & queen of the voodoo scene. My childhood was riddled with magic, spirituality and alternative forms of 'life' that were constantly lurking in the shadows as my parents used to say. This is what eventually made me develop a professional interest in the supernatural world, but I never truly believed in it.

Until I had an eerie dream about my late mother Madame Davina, sitting on a throne with my father's decaying corpse resting on her lap. She instructed me to come closer and told me that I had to go on a journey that would change the way I saw the entire world. At first, I chuckled but then I realized that mother was being serious, there was something about that dream that made me start believing in... 'The Other Side'?!

When I woke up from my hallucination I was no longer in my bed. But sitting on my desk, laptop fully logged on with an open webpage referring to directions from my house to the more secluded area of Deacon Valley.

It seemed like a very random destination with no actual connection to my fascination with occult studies. A simple, traditional American space, where people are unaware of the darker pitfalls of the world, as communal reasoning often takes the reins in these smalltown places.

But little did I know that I was headed on a journey that would later become the scariest weekend that I will ever experience in my entire life. An absolute rollercoaster full of twists, turns and death all across the board.

As I passed the welcome sign I could see it from afar, the vigil that was built in honor of Deshawn Davis. A young, promising Black man snatched by drug king pin Deandre Fredricks & sadly killed before the cops could save him. For once it wasn't them who tried to kill the innocent Black man, so I guess that's progress, in a way...

The only thing that doesn't sit right with me is; what was Deshawn doing with Deandre? Surely, as an honorary student and captain of the swimming team, he wouldn't associate himself with such a nasty individual? There has to be something greater at play here, there just has to be!

As I got closer to the vigil to pay my respects, I thought that tears would be running from my eyes before I even got out of my car. But it was quite the opposite, as soon as I parked, I felt a cold chill coursing all through my spine. It was almost as if I was touched by someone from beyond the veil of perception, a spirit of sorts...

I have already felt this feeling so many times before when I joined my mother in her religious ceremonies. Where subjects came to see her from all over the great Louisiana bayou, to be graced and healed by Madame Davina, the notorious Voodoo queen. Whenever I felt the chill, my mother told me to be wary of its presence, since it usually meant that a martyred spirit was not at peace and trying to communicate a message to a vessel.

I gathered enough courage to get out of my car, but as soon as I stepped out it felt like I wasn't alone. As if someone or something was watching me...

1.3 THE APPARITION OF DOOM

The vigil itself was so beautiful, the art students made a group sculpture honoring his athletic physique. Painted in full black and wearing a shiny BLM fist of resistance chain. Behind the statue a yearbook wall is filled with loving goodbye messages from his fellow students. It appears as though Deshawn was a real mister popular since everyone in school was sad to see him go.

So many messages of positivity and love, not even a single troll dared to write something bad about him. But there was one quote that stood out from everyone else's. Somehow I could feel the pain of the writer in the shaky lines of their writing on the wall. For some reason, it made a single tear run from my eye, since I was alone I spoke out the words to Deshawn's statue:

"Roses are red, violets are blue. How did I ever get so blessed to have shared my heart and soul with you?

Even though you're no longer here with me, I promise to never stop changing the world for everyone to see.

For our love knows no bounds not even that of life and death, that is why I'll hold on to you until my last breath.

Love, H.M."

Upon finishing the last sentence, the temperature suddenly dropped 20 degrees. I looked around and suddenly saw him standing there. An apparition whose presence is accompanied by nothing but death & destruction. He started coming closer to me & I immediately ran to my car, but I slipped and crashed to the ground, blacking out without a chance of saving myself from harm.

When I woke up, I immediately started screaming at the top of my lungs, eyes fully closed, completely unaware of my surroundings. Until I felt a sudden warm embrace that instantly shut down my voice. I opened my eyes to an older woman holding me in her arms while she kept promising me that I had nothing to worry about.

Moments later her husband approached, holding a hot cup of tea, offering it to me with a warm, disarming smile. They introduced themselves as Joseph & Lisa Maxwell. A retired law enforcement couple that chose to spend their final years at their cabin in the woods close to the valley's border. They talked about their greatest hits and I sat there and took in every story as a way of ignoring the blackout I just endured.

Then, the conversation shifted to me, as Lisa suddenly asked if I had remembered what happened. The question itself made my heart sink to my stomach, but I kept my poker face on, took a sip of my tea and calmly said that a general sense of grief got the best of me.

The Maxwells suddenly bowed their heads, as they were clearly at a loss for words. I asked them about Deshawn and apparently everyone in the valley saw him as a respectable teenager, flawless in every sense of the word.

Then came the question that ruined the peaceful mood; What was I doing in Deacon Valley? I truthfully told them about mother's message and they asked me to go without any explanation. I couldn't even thank them for their hospitality as they slammed the cabin door shut.

1.5 A TALE OF TWO DEMOGRAPHICS

As I'm driving to the motel for my check-in, I still can't seem to shake the Maxwell's reaction when I told them about the dream I had about my mother and her message. I expected them to laugh at me on the spot, but instead, they were shook by my answer. I knew something was up, I just had to figure out what it could possibly be.

For now, I'll just keep both my eyes and my ears wide open, who knows what clues might be connected to my mother's omen. I'm sure it won't be difficult to find clues since this Deacon Valley just seems way too... Stepfordy.

The lawns are too green, the 'cleanliness' is too forced and the people are way too composed. One ride to the motel and I can already tell that I'm stuck in yet another societal mindset where status, fakeness and the bitter, jaded common sense rule over the daily cycle of life.

Luckily, the motel I booked was in a secluded area away from the valley's main scene. As I got closer I noticed that the lawns got grayer, the streets more rugged and the people marched with neither hopes nor dreams. Just the piercing realization that there's no true escape for the endless drag that we all know as everyday life.

The last few miles were so quiet and peaceful, until I suddenly heard a police siren behind me. A cop car that literally came out of nowhere, gave me the signal to pull over and there were no witnesses around. I was sweating so hard while holding on to my steering wheel as if my life depended on it. Because history has proven that these encounters often don't end well for people like me.

I pulled over and waited for the officer to approach me, the seconds that it took him to step out of his car and walk towards me seemed like the longest hours of my life. I was in full panic mode, causing me to experience a severe internal dilation of both time and space.

As my surroundings seemed to fade away, leaving only the two of us present in the heat of the moment. He approached and left no room for small talk, "License & registration," he said in a calm tone with no sense of hostility. I was thrown off by the lack of violence, but I still managed to hand him my license without hesitation.

"You seem to be a long way from home." He uttered in a suspicious tone, I left no room for error and swiftly replied that I was visiting my family for my cousin's graduation. He seemed a bit suspicious of my answer but he remained silent, almost as if he was testing me. I made sure to show no sign of hesitation, for some reason staying calm in the face of danger seemed easy to me when the alternative was possible death at the hands of a cop.

He gave me back my license and told me to drive safe, I nodded and drove off at a calm pace, but my heart was racing, beating even faster than the speed of a bullet.

Upon arriving at the motel, there were a few red flags. The first was the empty parking lot, confirming that I was the only visitor. The second was the woman standing at the middle of the lot, as if she was eagerly waiting for me. My instinct was to turn around and drive away, but to my surprise I just stepped out with no hesitation.

1.7 THE PSYCHIC CONVERGENCE

She didn't move an inch as I kept walking closer, every instinct in body, mind and soul telling me to turn back and run to my car. But I kept walking until I faced her, she seemed completely unresponsive. I was about to move past her until she aggressively grabbed my hand.

"Ma Chérie,

I had no idea you would be confronted with The Apparition so soon. It appears his presence is more powerful than I first predicted.

But fear not my child, within the space of this motel you are safe from any harm. For the vessel that stands before you has blessed this soil with my magic.

I must go now, but we will meet again tonight, under different circumstances with another vessel.

All I can tell you is; be prepared... for the unprepared!"

Suddenly, the motel keeper let go of my hand and took a deep breath, as if she was gasping for air beyond measure. She smiled, nodded her head and grabbed my suitcase, as if my mother's spirit was still pulling her strings from beyond the grave. As she walked inside I was still completely shook by the craziness I just witnessed.

Even beyond the grave, Madame Davina is capable of explaining so much, without using too many words while still leaving no room for small talk nor questions. It appears I've gotten myself into some dark mess...

Once inside she started to check me in, what should've only been a few moments took forever. After a while I couldn't take it anymore so I got up to ask her about the delay. She replied that my room would be ready any minute now. She was simply making sure that the room would have everything I needed to help me on my journey, which simply made me feel even more suspicious.

The way she said it, so calm, with a hollow stare in her eyes made it clear to me that the motel keeper was still under mother's influence. So I let it go, sat back down and continued to wait through the boredom in absolute silence. Every passing second seeming so much longer because of everything I've already experienced today. A few minutes passed and she finally handed me the key with a smile on her face that screamed out 'fake'.

She gave me the key to room 101 upstairs on the far right side, I must say it's one of the cleanliest motel rooms I've stayed in. Nothing gives me the desire to shine a blacklight on the walls, so that's already a good sign. Once inside, I felt a wave of motherly protection take over my body, mind and soul. I know now why it took so long to get this room ready, as she made it into a safe haven full of protection charms blessed by my mother's energy, I could tell that this was her doing.

All I need now is some food, but sadly the motel is outside the scope of most restaurants that I passed on my way over here. Except for one, "The Rapid Valley", a small fast-food place with zero reviews because they just started deliveries today; I guess it was just meant to be...

1.9 A DINNER OF SOLITUDE

It was the shortest wait time I've ever had, almost as if they were desperate to receive my order. I'm already questioning the quality of my food as I hear the delivery guy pulling up to the motel. By the sound of the steps I could tell that he was not a small man.

As he got closer to my room I already walked outside and shut the door to avoid any awkward misunderstandings. He greeted me from afar, while holding my pizza & wings in one hand, and his phone in the other.

As he got closer he took a sudden, deep breath and dropped everything, including my order. I couldn't even get mad at him because I clearly saw that his reaction came from a genuine place of shock.

Before I could even ask him what happened he picked up my food and apologized. I asked him what caused this 'reaction' and he showed me his phone, from the headline alone I knew why he was shook. The Maxwells were murdered in cold blood not far from their cabin.

From the look in the big man's eyes it was clear to me that his shock came from a place of relief. He was truly happy to see them dead, and when I asked him about it all he said was; "What goes around comes around!".

Apparently the kindness I experienced from them was not this Black man's experience. He could tell I wanted to know more so he blocked me and took off without even giving me his name. Apparently he's not the vessel who would make my mother's spirit reappear to me...

At the very least my food was still edible after that clumsy drop, and even though it was bomb I simply couldn't enjoy it. I finished it way too fast as I was busy eating through all of my feelings of anxiety.

During the process of stuffing my face I scrolled through every corner of the internet to find out why The Maxwell's were dealt such a deadly hand. But I was unsuccessful as they seemed squeaky clean, almost too clean. I know it'll only be a matter of time before I find the actual reason behind this act of violence.

I wanted nothing more than to put away my phone and go to sleep, but I couldn't do that before my mother visited me again. If I dared to fall asleep now it would most definitely trigger a tragedy stricken nightmare that cursed the overwhelming majority of my youth.

I turned on the little TV and as fate would have it, new details regarding the assassination had been released. The Maxwell's were forced into their police uniforms and were killed by a weapon that they carried for 35 years of service; a 9 mm Beretta. Next to their bodies they found a dark-skinned female blow-up doll wearing a red dress with a name written on it; "Gina Ramirez".

Apparently she was a single mother who passed away a long time ago and had ties to several gangs. When I looked up the name of her orphaned son it turned out to be the delivery man that was here earlier, much to my surprise. Could it be that he was glad to see them killed because his mom died under 'suspicious' circumstances?

NO JUSTICE
NO PEACE
BLM

CHAPTER 2:

To Match A Description.

Narrator: Dylan Maxwell

"There's no book to figure out how not to become a victim of police brutality."

Mike Colter

2.1 SLEEPING WITH EYES WIDE OPEN

Apparently Madame Davina's power of premonition is not as effective from the grave, for in about ten minutes or so it'll be midnight and I still haven't seen another vessel that would trigger her spirit to show up. I guess mother won't be joining for a late night chat session after all. So now all I have to do is figure out a way to get some sleep before my journey starts tomorrow.

Normally, I just have to close my eyes and I'm gone for the night, but somehow I just can't seem to let go of my thoughts. Everything that happened today was just too much to process, my mind is stuck on repeat. For some reason everything from the apparition, to the Maxwells and the delivery guy all seem tied to a greater story. If that's true, then what the hell did I get myself into?

I've been on many journeys before & have faced many dangerous mysteries, but somehow this one feels like it may actually mean the end of me. I laid on my bed and kept staring at the ceiling, desperately trying to find my brain's reset button. Seconds seemed to pass by like minutes making an actual minute feel like an entire hour had passed. For a while, it seemed hopeless until it all suddenly stopped! The memories of today that I kept replaying in my head were gone and the manipulative voice in my head that fuels my anxiety was silenced.

My eyes were still wide open but my mind was no longer present in the moment. The smudged white ceiling I was staring at started to turn into an image, as if an acid trip was creating a magical painting. A painting of a protest full of violent conflict without a chance for resolution.

AN ANCESTRAL HALLUCINATION 2.2

As soon as the painting on the ceiling was finished it lured me in and sent me to a dreamscape. Suddenly, I was in the 60's, marching alongside the pioneers of the Civil Rights Movement. Walking for a better tomorrow while continuing to endure the tragic struggles of today.

I've already been to several marches before but none of them compared to this one. The level of purity and sincerity that resonated from our human connection was unparalleled. Everyone here was actually marching for change, rather than using Justice & Equality as a way to chase online clout under the guise of 'activism'. Bringing forth a wave of allies that were destined to at some point take their goal too far and pass their place.

That was definitely not the vibe here, I felt so protected, empowered and determined to march until both of my feet were blistered and my voice was gone. Everyone would hear my chanting for a new world where the injustices of this one would finally be left in the past.

But my subconscious mind had other plans, as my surroundings instantly started to change. Day turned into night the same way the crowded city streets became an abandoned field with no other life in sight. There I stood all alone, scared & stuck with only one way out, an underground tunnel so dark you can't even see the light at the end, so that's why there's a flashlight at the entrance.

Normally I'd never even consider going inside, but a sudden cold shiver & a look across my shoulder made it clear that the apparition was also here so I ran inside!

2.3 A TUNNEL OF BODIES

This acid trip really was starting to feel like a horror movie! I ran inside the tunnel, guns blazing before I could even turn on the flashlight. While in full sprint mode I kept pushing the on/off button but the light just kept flickering the entire time until it just shut off.

So I guess running as if my life depended on it was the only remaining option for me. It didn't take long for the light at the end to appear and as soon as it caught my eye all I could think of was reaching the end so I could finally escape this deadly nightmare. For a second, it almost seemed like I'd make it, until my stupid clumsiness got the best of me yet again as I fell face first to the ground.

Luckily, I still had the flashlight firmly gripped in my hand. Apparently, the fall wasn't all bad because at the very least it made the flickering stop so I could finally see the inside of the tunnel. At first glance, it seemed to be your average, run of the mill creepy, dark tunnel that would terrify any normal human being. But then I realized something was wrong after a sudden, vile smell.

The smell was so bad, it almost seemed like a corpse was rotting not that far from where I was standing. Sadly, I turned out to be right as a dead body suddenly dropped from the ceiling of the tunnel. I had no idea who it could be as the body was in such a decomposed state that it made most zombies look like cheerleaders.

All I really knew was that it grabbed my leg as soon as I aimed the flashlight at its face! Naturally, all I could really do was violently kick it in the face and run for dear life.

All I could think of was running, running until my legs could run no more. Running until I reached that light at the end of the tunnel. As I got closer, more and more dead bodies started to pop up out of nowhere. When I ran past them, they resurrected just in time to grab my legs, in an attempt to trip me. But this time around, I was determined not to fall or I would be done for.

As I got closer, I realized the light was a portal to a different dream dimension, normally I'd stop and think twice before going through it. But under these circumstances there's no chance in hell I'm staying here, I gave everything I had in a final sprint and jumped in.

The journey through the portal passed by so fast I don't even remember it, all I can remember was my sigh of relief to be out of that creepy tunnel. On the other side, I found myself in a field once again, but this time around there was no apparition there and I also had company. A beautiful dark-skinned woman with long, wavy natural curls wearing a bright red dress with matching heels.

She was laying on the ground while she kept staring at the moon who had just reached its full potential. In this form, the planet almost resembles a facial expression looking down at us with a bright shimmer that lights up the stars in its vicinity. I slowly got closer and laid down next to her so I could ask who she was. "You already know who I am my dear, as you already met my son" she replied in a warm, friendly tone. I didn't even have to ask her who she was as I could see the resemblance between her and the delivery guy from earlier today.

2.5 A SWEATY AWAKENING

I instantly had so many questions to ask her but she stopped me before I could even begin.

"I'm afraid your time in this dreamscape has reached its end my dear, time to go back to reality.

Once you wake up, you will meet your mother soon enough, just make sure to wait for her in the lobby.

There will simply be one more hurdle to cross before she appears, I can assure you it will make the fear you've experienced just now seem like a loving embrace.

If you could please do me one favor when you return to the land of the living?"

I reluctantly agreed to let my questioning go and nodded my head to answer her question. She smiled and deeply stared in my eyes, hoping I'd understand.

"When you meet my son again, tell him I could never be prouder to have a child like him. For he truly held on to all of the values that I taught him as a little boy.

And even though the system may have failed him, he never failed himself because he promised me that he'd make something of himself, and he did!"

Her message was so sincere, it made my heart melt as I saw a tear run from her left-eye. She put her hand on my forehead and suddenly everything went dark. When I opened my eyes again, I woke up sweaty and confused.

I had just taken three separate journeys all in the same dreamscape, it seemed like hours had gone by but when I look at my clock it was only one minute. I was only out for 60 seconds but it felt so long, it's giving me alternate universes at this point. If only I could've stayed a little longer to hear her story, that would've helped me figure out why she was involved in the death of The Maxwells. How the hell do I find out any of the business now?

But, it also seemed like I was destined to wake up at this time because my phone had just blown up with notification alerts. Apparently, a video has been released of the murder earlier tonight. The video was made by the killer himself, a man who calls himself The Beast Of Liberty.

One quick Internet search and I found his manifesto of terror with only one mission in life. To bring forth justice in its most brutal form, without ever feeling its own consequences. That seems to be his way of receiving reparations for everything that our ancestors went through in the United States of America and the world..

He was wearing sneakers, jeans and a hoodie, his face hidden behind a Guy Fawkes mask adapted with symbols that praise blackness itself, it seems The Maxwells had gotten Gina killed a long time ago. Due to their flawless record no one thought that any foul play was involved so they just let it go as yet another unfortunate circumstance. And they were about to get away with it and live out the rest of their days in peace and tranquility, but the beast had other ideas and somehow I get the feeling they're only the first victims on his long list…

2.7 DRIFTING IN THE MOTEL LOBBY

I put on my coat and shoes, got out of my room and went to the lobby. There was no one there so I assumed the motel keeper went home or stayed in one of the other rooms. I had no idea and I was not planning on finding out either. All I did was sit on the chair and wait for something to happen, no matter how long it'd take.

At least that's what I've gathered from everything I've just experienced. I'm pretty sure mother was on her way right now, the only question that's left was; Who the hell was this different vessel that she was referring to ?

Could it be the delivery guy? Maybe he had a dream about his mother too and wants to talk about it? Or maybe it's someone else? Like a town elder or one of the many faces I passed on my way over here. Either way, I'll wait until the vessel in question showed up.

The first minute came and no one showed, then came the second minute still no one to be seen and there it was, on the 3rd minute I heard a car approaching. I had no idea who he could be until I saw the police lights through the window. The vessel my mother was referring to was Dylan Maxwell, the officer who pulled me over and whose parents were killed by The Beast Of Liberty.

Today truly was a day full of scary, destiny stricken co-incidences. He seemed very rushed as if he wanted to get out of here as soon as possible. As he got out of his car, he saw me through the window and signaled me to come out. Normally I'd be scared to death but I knew my mother consecrated these grounds to keep me safe.

Once I walked outside, he wasted no time and directly went in. He told me that he went to his parent's cabin and that they'd left a note for him warning them of me and what my intentions were. They even got my physical description matched to a tee, I never would have guessed that given how quickly they kicked me out after I was honest. Weirdly, Dylan didn't seem to be mourning their death, it almost felt like he knew it was coming, like he was happy to be able to hold on to them for so long.

He was calm, direct and spoke with zero emotional tone in his voice, I was completely thrown off as I was expecting anger, tears and borderline aggression. But instead I got a dry, stoic personality that wasn't going to let me go until I gave him what he wanted. The only problem was that I was clueless as to why this tragedy mysteriously started when I entered Deacon valley.

But just like that the calm went away, apparently that was just strategy, because the very second I became a nuisance his entire mood shifted. He started to yell, got in my face and tried to intimidate me in every single way imaginable but I was determined not to let him get to me. I stayed calm and kept saying that I knew nothing because I literally knew nothing, in my mind I'm still shocked as to why my mother chose to send me here.

I said no too many times, because the abusive cop persona suddenly popped up, he was aiming for his police radio as if he was going to call in this 'incident'. I panicked, tried to interrupt him and just like that I became a 'threat' so he took out his gun & aimed it at my head.

2.9 TO BE HELD AT GUNPOINT

They say your life flashes before your eyes when you're about to die, reliving your greatest hits like a show reel containing the good, the bad and the truth behind every single lie. But that was not the case for me, All I could do was panic and hide my fear so I wouldn't give him a sense of winning. I hope this means that there was still a place for my soul in the realm of the living.

There he stood, angry, aggressive and drunk on all sorts of unjustified power, yelling at me to give him what he wants, or else... My mind was going a mile a minute, I was begging for my mother to show up, hoping that a spiritual glitch was the reason for her delayed appearance. As he kept growing more impatient, I realized I had to figure out a way to stall him long enough for my mother to show up and rescue me from this danger.

I told him that the answer was in my motel room, he stared me down for a second as if he didn't believe me. But it's not like he had much of an option, so eventually he agreed and told me to lead the way. With every step I begged my mother to show up, there was so much sweat dripping off my forehead, even more intensely than the longest deadliest marathon that I could ever run.

As we got closer to the room, my panic levels had already reached a critical overload. I stopped in front of my door and just froze out of sheer sense of panic, there was nothing I could do that could get me out of this. That's when his impatience suddenly got the better of him as he pulled his 9mm beretta back out, but this time, he actually put it directly against my temple.

I truly can't explain how awful it was to feel that cold metal against my skin, I was absolutely petrified, my body was rock solid, no scary shakiness whatsoever as my mind had already left the building. I truly thought this was going to my last living moment on earth.

But just like that, Madame Davina arrived to rescue me from this evil fool. Suddenly, the hand that held the gun started to shake intensely, by his shocked facial expression I could tell that the shaking wasn't his doing. The gun moved away from my temple, and slowly moved towards his own as he hopelessly tried to resist it. As soon as it made contact with his skin, he shut his eyes and when he reopened them I knew it was mom.

"Apologies for the delay ma chérie, it was far more difficult than I Imagined to cross the veil at this hour.

Fear not, for I'm wiping this vessel's memory as we speak, he will have no recollection of you nor the profile description that his parents made of you.

This mind-wipe spell will last for as long as the note remains in your possession. If you fear it won't be possible to keep it with you, then you must burn it in the presence of someone that he's wronged. Now grab the note from his left-side pocket so he can finally leave."

I did what she asked and suddenly Dylan put the gun back in his holster and started walking back to his car. While I simply stood there completely traumatized and unable to process the crazy mess that I just witnessed.

NO JUSTICE
NO PEACE
BLM

CHAPTER 3:

To Be Shaken Upside Down.

Narrator: Jasmine Davis

"Racism is still with us. But it's up to us to prepare our children for what they have to meet & hopefully, we shall overcome."

Rosa Parks

3.1 SLEEPING IN SHORT CYCLES

It felt like I was a giraffe trying to get some kind of rest in the open woodlands of Africa, sleeping with one eye open in short cycles of half an hour. Terrified of what else the night may bring with it, and how I would respond to even more crazy things happening to me.

Every half hour I would wake up screaming, while my clothes were drenched in sweat. I kept praying to fall asleep until morning would come, as I can't possibly explain the overwhelming feelings of anxiety every time I looked around my room. Even the protection charms surrounding every inch of this safe space felt like a mere hoax meant to ease my paralyzing fear.

It seemed hopeless for me to get a good night's rest, so after the third awakening I stopped trying altogether. At the very least I had my phone with me to pass the time, I figured I may as well do some work right now. I started a social media investigation to find out more about The Maxwell couple and their shocking death.

Based on the comments of the news report explaining their untimely demise, it became clear that those two were not at all like the good Samaritans who helped me when I found myself in supernatural trouble.

So it's really not that shocking that their son Dylan was such an aggressive nightmare, as the apple rarely falls far from the extremely disturbing tree. Then I found a comment from an anonymous user, "finally justice will be served to Deacon Valley". Upon reading it, my lights went out as if I was in a magical sleeping spell.

A FINAL DREAMSCAPE REVISITED 3.2

When I woke up from that brief knockout, I found myself back at the field where I briefly met Gina. The beautiful Afro-Latina that was taken from this world long before it was her time to go. But this time around she wasn't alone, her son was also there and even though he was just a little boy, the resemblance to his adult version whom I had met earlier today truly was uncanny.

They were just rolling around and playing in the grass, having the greatest time of their life, as if they didn't have a care in the world, all that mattered was having fun and putting a smile on her little boy's face. Young, adorable little Gabriel Ramirez, with stylish, baggy clothes and that big, curly mess of a hairstyle that his mom was so proud of as she ran her hands through it.

I tried to get closer to them but for some weird reason the distance between us kept growing as I continued to move. It was almost like an invisible barrier had been placed between us so we wouldn't be able to interact with one another. I grew tired of walking so I started to run towards them, the distance stopped growing and finally I was successfully able to approach them.

But I truly wish I hadn't as they flagged me as a threat, Gabriel was so terrified he hid behind his mother who was giving me the stare of death. Before I could even let them know that they were safe from harm, Gina screamed and her body turned into a ghostly figure that was coming right at me full force. It all happened so fast that it completely stopped me in my tracks, I was unable to run, hide or even try to defend myself...

3.3 BREAKFAST IN THE PARKING LOT

As I felt her spirit transfer through mine, I woke up from my dream, when I stared at the window I realized the sun had arrived bringing with it a brand new dawn.

I hopped in the shower and instantly started scrubbing away all of the traumatic and bizarre experiences that I came across in the last 24 hours. In my mind I thought if I scrubbed hard enough I could truly wash away the memories from my mind the same way that I could wash away the dirt on my skin. It didn't take me long to figure out that there's no such thing, once an experience sets in your mind there's truly no undoing both the physical and psychological damage that comes along with it.

Once I felt as clean as I possibly could be, I dried myself, got dressed and went back to the lobby. I dreaded every single step I took towards the lobby entrance, since every step reminded me of how awful it felt to have a gun against my temple with no real guarantee of protection.

I was almost there until that damn motel keeper suddenly walked outside with a smile so wide it seemed like she was up to something sketchy. I looked her in the eyes, smiled back to her but stayed suspicious about her true intentions as I always knew better than most people.

She pointed her hand to the left and when I turned my head, I saw a beautifully decorated picknick table at the center of the empty parking lot. With a beautiful spread of many different breakfast delights. "I prepared a special breakfast for you today" she said to me in a tone so calm and happy it came across very disturbing to me.

Oh how I dreaded the idea of having to eat with Nora the motel keeper, a woman I can only describe as sketchy due to her freakishly optimistic nature. It's so damn extra all of the time that I can't even begin to process her true intentions. But luckily, Nora said she had to go run an 'errand', whatever the hell that's supposed to mean.

Either way, I was going to be able to enjoy breakfast in peace so I could get myself together, or at least try as hard as I could to come close enough. Because my instincts were warning me, that the craziness of last night was only the beginning of a very wild ride.

There's no way Nora did all of this by herself, as only my mother would know to set up the picknick table far away from the tire tracks left behind by Dylan's dangerous visit last night. It may seem subtle and random but I still had my belief it was her doing. So for a brief moment, I didn't even think about last night's trauma as I was just focusing on the taste of the deliciously prepared food.

But apparently I'm never allowed to catch a break since mayhem has found me yet again, I was suddenly approached by a distraught woman. I had no idea who she was but judging by the uniform she was wearing I could tell that he belonged to the housekeeping staff.

What really threw me off was the way she looked at me, it almost appeared as if she had seen a ghost of her past. She sat down and stared deeply into my eyes, the silent stare really threw me off, I decided to bite and asked her who the hell she was but I wasn't ready for her answer...

3.5 CONSOLING A MOTHER'S PAIN

"I had a dream about you last night, you were even wearing the same outfit you're wearing right now.

It was the first time I've been able to dream about something other than my boy Deshawn being taken away from me long before it was his time to pass.

This has to mean something, it just has to!

Please, tell me who you are, leave no details out whatsoever, I want to hear your entire story!"

Apparently, I wasn't the only one tripping hells bells last night, I do believe it means something that she saw me in the dream world. I think it means that she's the next stop on my journey towards the truth I have to uncover.

The fact that she's Deshawn's mother only confirms that assumption even more, maybe she can provide some intel regarding the apparition that scared the crap out of me at the memorial yesterday. I knew there was no way she would ever be an open book with me if I didn't flip open my cover first. So I did and before I could even get to the juicy part she interrupted me…

"Is your mother Madame Davina?"

I was shook, but I nodded my head to give my answer.

"Then, I guess I should call you my niece, since she was my estranged sister. I wish we could've met under better circumstances but I'm glad you're here anyway."

My grandfather Lucien Monroe had left my grandmother Lucille whom I'm named after and their daughter Davina, A.K.A. mom, for a younger woman named Linda with whom he made little Jasmine not long after.

Suddenly, my life seemed like a NOLA voodoo inspired telenovela, ripe with intrigue, drama and betrayal as if it was written in the modern day. This plot twist just can't be real? I have to still be dreaming, stuck in another dimension where reality seems so far, far away?

As she continued to talk about her childhood I started to think that this is the reason I'm here, so that both Jasmine and I could connect and heal by finding solace in each other's pain. Next time I see my mother I'll ask her why she never told me anything about her childhood.

As aunt Jasmine was no help with that given the fact that she had only met my mother once at their father Lucien's funeral, and neither of their mothers let them interact with each other, further straining their relationship.

For all of their lives they had to know about each other's existence without actually knowing, no cellphones with easy call access and no social media profiles to stalk every aspect of each other's lives while pretending not to care about each other's business at all.

Maybe they felt the same way I do at this moment since I never got to meet my cousin Deshawn, I wonder what kind of boy he was and what kind of man he could have been had he not been taken from this world.

3.7 A WALK DOWN MEMORY LANE

Suddenly she stopped talking about her childhood and she started having flashbacks to the night of Deshawn's death. Something must have triggered her memory but I had no idea what it could be, all I could do was hold her hand and let her know she could talk to me if she needed someone that would listen to her.

She appreciated it, but all she really wanted was one day where she could feel the relief of not carrying around such a heavy chest due to her unfixable broken heart.

If only there was a way for me to help her achieve this goal, but I doubt it's even possible. I doubt any person can ever truly get over the loss of a loved one, but surely nothing compares to the pain of a mother losing a child?

A life that she made so many sacrifices for, only to have it stripped away from her before she could start to enjoy the fruits of her hard labor. The mystery of life often does seem like a cruel joke, with the undeniable reality that we can lose it any moment as its morbid punchline.

I asked her how she gets through the day and her answer made me sick to my stomach, to the point that I actually threw up all of the breakfast delights I consumed.

"Officer Dylan often visits me so I can release my pain.

He even drove me back home the day of Deshawn's death as I left my house barefoot and mind boggled.

He did his best, but sadly my son's body remains cold."

Now I understand why my mother sent me here, I have to help my aunt Jasmine find peace with her son's death while also making sure that the ones who are truly responsible are brought to justice. The only mystery that truly remains is that of The Beast Of Liberty and how he factors in the greater story. Clearly he's not an apparition unless they've suddenly developed the ability to materialize and record deadly performances?

He has to be a human being connected to this somehow, because the idea that it's just a coincidental mystery is just way too much of a reach. Normally I'm pretty good at keeping things to myself, but this time I just couldn't after hearing that Dylan was the one who handled the paperwork for Deshawn's death. I felt like I owed it to my aunt to tell her what happened last night, even if it would tear her soul apart, it was the right thing to do.

As I told her my story she stared at me with open eyes as if the endless pieces of this tragic puzzle were finally starting to fit into a greater story. The story of a police cover-up to hide yet another injustice that's happened way too many times before in our history. Even though I don't have a shred of proof I know that's what happened. I just know it in my heart and so did she.

Aunt Jasmine completely lost it, threatening to drive to the police station so she could kill Dylan herself. but luckily she was willing to respond to reason. So I was able to talk her down because of it. Not long after that, she burst into tears as I held her in my arms trying my very best to console her hopelessly broken spirit.

3.9 THE CURSE OF RAISING A CHILD

She spent 10 minutes crying but it seemed like an eternity of pain was flowing through her teary eyes, each aching sound she made further fueling my empathy for her. I had no idea how I was going to do it, but I would move rivers and mountains to make sure her troubled and broken spirit could finally start to move on.

I held her in my arms as tight as I could, giving her the idea that I would never let go. I could tell that she truly appreciated it as she held on to me even tighter. It truly felt like she was trying to hug her sister through me.

But all I could think of was the pain that a sudden blood member felt and how devastating it must be to birth and raise a child in this truly and utterly disturbing world. You give everything you have to give, you break your mind, your body and your soul to make sure that they can have everything that you never did as a child.

All so that they may one day look back and think about you with nothing but love and respect for the sacrifices that you made. But unfortunately, nothing in this life was ever guaranteed as in this case aunt Jasmine outlived her own son which is a tragic reality that no mother on this planet should ever have to go through.

By the sound of her cries I could tell that there was no coming back from this, no matter how hard she would try to heal, the scars of her son's death simply ran far too deep. All I could really do to help her, was find the evidence that would expose the truth, consequences be damned for me and the rest of this sketchy valley.

The tears suddenly stopped and aunt Jasmine shot up while her body started to shiver intensely. She had a blank stare in her eyes, and turned her head towards me as her body started to stabilize again.

"Ma Chérie, I'm glad everything's going the way I planned, now you know why I sent you here.

Even though I never had a relationship with her, my soul can't be at peace without bringing her justice.

With my guidance you will call upon a seance, so you can summon your nephew's spirit for a limited time.

But first, you must go back to the vigil, and bring back the broken man who can't seem to leave his memory.

As without him, there is no seance to be performed, go on my child. For my sister and I still have many things to discuss inside her mind before we can continue."

Before I could even respond to her cryptic message, aunt Jasmine's vessel instantly had her lights turned off.

At first, I hesitated to leave her behind, but then came motel keeper Nora out of nowhere yet again! She helped her up and surprisingly already had a wheelchair ready.

I guess that was the errand that she had to run earlier, it seems my mother truly is running this ship. But to what extent? And how much of it can she truly control given the fact that last night's intervention was a real close call.

NO JUSTICE
NO PEACE
BLM

CHAPTER 4:

To See Your Inner Evil.

Narrator: Darius Davis

"When men sow the wind it is rational to expect that they will reap the whirlwind."

Frederick Douglass

4.1 A VENGEFUL SPIRIT REVISITED

This is the very first time in my adult life that I wished to hit every red light on my route. As I wanted to delay my arrival as much as I possibly could, for the very idea that I would meet the apparition again made my heart sink to my stomach while my anxiety got the best of me.

Is it Deshawn's spirit? Or a mere shapeshifter seeking to emulate my nephew's essence with a devious presence? Whatever the answer, it creeped me out and I hope he doesn't show himself this time around. In my mind, I was praying that I could be in and out within the blink of an eye. Once I arrive, I step out of my car, retrieve the desired subject and drive off without looking back.

That was the ideal outcome that I was praying for, but there was no way that would actually happen given the fact that nothing will go my way on this journey. In reality, I would have to face difficulties on multiple levels. The first one being the apparition and the second the desired subject whom I doubt will go with me without feeling like something sketchy was going on.

As I got closer, a little voice in my head kept telling me to keep on driving even after I had reached the vigil sign. As if a part of me wanted to leave the mystery and danger of this valley behind me, even though I haven't even been here for a full 24 hours.

If the blood-line link hadn't been exposed, then I most certainly would've left. But even though I don't really know aunt Jasmine and Deshawn, I still feel like its my duty to stand my ground and bring them justice.

As I was about to pull up to the vigil, I didn't even have time to mentally prepare myself as a loud scream instantly triggered my instincts. A scream so desperate and scary it could only mean that someone's life was in danger. There was no time to park, I simply stopped the car and ran out to seek out the soul in need of saving, so unaware that I could be blindly walking into a trap.

Once I arrived at the vigil, I saw the apparition hovering over a distraught man lying on the ground that desperately tried to look away while screaming out in pain. The shock from that Deja Vu moment made me slip and I also fell, this made the apparition turn and focus on me.

I was so scared at that moment that I couldn't move, it approached until it started to hover over me. Unlike the man who was still freaking out, I was simply petrified. I watched as the apparition hovered, and somehow it no longer seemed like a danger to me. It was like I knew him this time around, it truly was my nephew.

In a leap of faith, I was able to lift up my arm and hold it out to him, he then did the same and as we felt each other's touch it almost created a psychic bond between us. A few seconds later Deshawn's spirit vanished and I was able to get back up without any trouble at all.

I walked over to the broken man and as I saw his face he seemed so familiar even though I never met him. He has to be connected to Deshawn somehow, I leaned down and got closer as he finally opened his eyes and saw me, he leaned on me and started to weep like a sad child.

4.3 THE SINGLE MOM EXPERIENCE

By the heartbreaking cries he kept making out towards Deshawn it didn't take me long to figure out that he was the father. Darius Davis, a man who can only be described as an absolute success in his professional life and an abject failure in his private one. As he is currently on his second divorce with no hope for reconciliation.

He had met aunt Jasmine when they were just teenagers about to embark on their freshman year at an HBCU. It was love at first sight, that eventually turned into a toxic mess of a relationship that was only made worse when auntie found out that she was pregnant with twins.

She had to drop out to take of the twins while he got to stay and finish his education. It all seemed like it would work out in the end, until he bailed after graduation. To begin a new life, as the old one was simply too much of a rough patch for his goals in the future.

Aunt Jasmine had to work two jobs, just so she could put food on the table for Deshawn and Shaniece. All while taking care of them without ever being given a chance to take care of herself. And like the ultimate boss woman she was, she actually made it work.

When the twins got older she even went back to school, finished her degree in psychology and actually helps in the community center now. Attempting to support the ones in her community who are desperately in need of it, but too afraid to ask given the societal stigma surrounding mental health. But now who will be there to heal her broken heart? Or will be she looked over yet again?

After a while, he stopped crying and stared in front of him with a facial expression so lost and confused. It almost seemed like he was no longer on planet earth, but rather buried in a time loop of his own regretful memories. I could clearly see two things in his eyes, the first was the guilt that he struggled with due to his invisible presence as a father and a coparent.

The second was the admiration that he had for his ex-wife and everything she persevered through due to his inability to step up and take care of his responsibilities. She was able to be both a father and a mother to their children, and even though she did the best she could, it was normal that the absence of Darius had a deep & profound impact on both Deshawn & Shaniece's development as kids. It was clear because the first few years he still used to visit them and play with them, but as time moved on so did his desire to still be a present father figure in the lives of his children from a previous marriage.

For a new love interest came along and he saw a chance to rebuild and start over with his desires, as if he could just do away with his past and start again with a blank slate for the future. I'll never understand the braindead psyche of a man and in particular how his brain functions. How on earth can you possibly build up so much audacity and arrogance to think that you can simply wipe your hands clear from such a major responsibility? All because you weren't biologically designed to birth children and because society doesn't expect you to sacrifice everything just so you can provide the necessary care for them, it truly is no wonder why this world is such a mess.

4.5 A FRESH START REFLEX

The sad reality is that a lot of men share this particular character trait, the idea that they have the privilege to obtain a clean slate. While the woman is forever tainted in society's eyes as a single mom dumb enough to choose the wrong man who simply wanted to hit it and quit it.

Many of the men that try to court us probably don't even want a family life. But simply go along with it because they're too scared to be their true selves so they just go through life in their privileged social construct.

How can one just turn around and walk away while pretending to look back a few times to give off the idea that your children's well-being is important. But in reality it never crosses their mind, it's just something that hits you deep when you see that the damage has been done with no possible chance of repair. So it gets stuffed deep inside their tainted soul, buried under a vessel of absolute fakeness so the public image remains flawless.

What did these children do to deserve a lifetime of wondering why they weren't good enough to have their father stay in their lives? What evil did they bring upon us adults, as being born wasn't even their choice to begin with. I'll never be able to understand this, and a part of me hopes that Darius never forgives himself for his actions. Because in reality, any man who performs this type of abandonment doesn't deserve to be forgiven.

And to make things even worse when I asked him if he ever thought about being a part of their lives again, his reply pissed me off so much I wanted to slap him silly.

"Not a day went by that I didn't think about them, but I figured the damage was already done.

So I thought I'd make it up to them when they got older.

By then we would all have the shared experience of growing up without a father figure in our lives.

But never in a million years did I ever think that I would outlive one of my children.

And now it's simply too late to..."

And BOOM, there go the waterworks as he starts weeping like a child all over again. His answer really floored me, I couldn't even bring myself to fake a sense of empathy. He was in serious pain and actually deserved to be feeling this way, no doubt about it whatsoever.

And even if I tried to make him feel better by comforting him, he would still find himself stuck in a bottomless pit of absolute self-loathing. While attacking him would be even more useless given the fact that whatever I say or do to him could never compare to the damage he will do to himself for the rest of his regretful days.

Never will he find salvation from his troubled soul, even if the underlying truth is exposed, it would do nothing to make him feel better. All he can really do is hope that his daughter Shaniece is willing to give him a chance to rebuild their relationship. Maybe he can use that newly rekindled bond to find some form of inner peace.

4.7 THE DEADLY PLOT TWIST

As old man Darius continued to cry tears of absolute sorrow, Deshawn's spirit suddenly reappeared. This time around I could clearly see his face and what a beautiful young man he was. He smiled at me and held out his arm, I didn't think twice about it and leaned in to hold his hand. As soon as we touched, it sent me to another dreamscape where I was in a children's room. Where a giant clock firmly stood still on June 19, 2023 at 20h30.

Based on my internet research the night before, I remembered that this was the exact time that the 911 dispatch received the distress call that came before his untimely demise. I was suspicious of the entire vibe and then I heard some footsteps approaching.

Not long after, two figures entered, it was Darius and a little boy so full of joy. His name decorated in a large font on the side of the wall where his cute but extra car shaped bed takes over half the room. Little Demetrius Davis, his son and half-brother to Aunt Jasmine's twins. There was such a strong bond of absolute love between these two, I could feel it radiate through my entire body even though I wasn't actually there.

He held Demetrius in his arms and gently kissed him on his forehead before tucking him in. He didn't even need a bedtime story as his lights went out pretty fast, and he would remain that way for as long as Darius stayed by his side. Only after he falls into a deep slumber is it safe for him to leave the room, so Darius always made sure to keep his phone with him. But this time around he probably wished that he left it downstairs...

He was scrolling carelessly through every single one of his social media, passing the time until it was safe for him to go downstairs. His son twisting & turning in his bed, always moving around one of his hands to check for his father's presence. While Darius always made sure that his hand was on the top left side of the bed so his son could always reach out to him without getting up.

It couldn't have been more than a few minutes of scrolling until he received 'the message'. It was a simple, cold and dry message written to him by aunt Jasmine, as if she felt like he didn't have the right to a more detailed history. Which I could understand given the fact that Darius was more of a sperm & financial donor to his twins, rather than a present and positive father figure. Since he had clearly failed his first test of fatherhood!

After reading it, he felt a panic attack coming up while his heart was beating faster than the speed of any light. He wanted to scream out in absolute pain over the loss of Deshawn, but he also wanted to keep Demetrius from his needed night's rest. So he could try to live vicariously through his son's dreams to escape the eternally painful truth of his tragic reality as a mourning father.

He just sat there in absolute silence while the voices in his head were screaming with a loud piercing sound so explosive it could make you suffer from a stroke. He tried his very best to stay quiet but couldn't help the vast stream of tears flooding from his unprepared eyes. He continued to sit there until his son was finally in a deep sleep, so he could go downstairs and fully break down.

4.9 A MESSAGE GONE VIRAL

I didn't even get to see his breakdown, as a sudden disruption of loud, beeping sounds instantly ended the tragic setting of the dreamscape. I then found myself in a hollow space with nothing but brightly colored wires, all tangled together to create an intertwined stream of connection. All the while the beeping sounds continue to echo throughout this mystical space as if it was trying to speak to me in a language I was unable to understand.

At first, I thought I was stuck in the most abstract, linear parts of my brain, it wasn't that much of a reach after all, given the extremely messy chaos I endured recently. Maybe my mind simply had enough, as if it preferred to shut down completely rather than continue with this disturbingly unreal journey. But then, I realized this had to do with the real world, something happened when I phased out to witness this flashback. As soon as I made that realization I was launched back into the real world.

Darius had stopped crying in the meantime, his phone gripped tightly in his hands as he can't stop staring at the screen in shock. I approached and saw a teenage girl whispering to her phone, she was in a bathroom live streaming what she called a 'copaganda' invasion.

I could tell by her heavy breathing that her heart was racing, but she was able to hold her composure. When I asked Darius who she was he ignored me. I had to ask several times before he finally acknowledged me and answered my question which left my mouth wide open.

"She's my daughter, Deshawn's younger twin sister..."

We kept staring at the screen and sending her messages to check on her, she hesitated at first but then let it slip where she was. As soon as she said that she and a bunch of her friends were being held in school we both got up without hesitation and ran towards our cars. Darius led the way as I trailed him while following the livestream.

Apparently, the mask that The Beast Of Liberty uses was made by a group of student activists in school called The Justice Collective. It was inspired by the worldwide protests from the Black Lives Matter movement seeking to enforce **Justice** so we may finally know what it feels like to be at **Peace**. Surely, no one is dumb enough to believe that an angry, loud student with a passion for social & moral justice would be able to commit such a deadly crime? I know that's just bull, they're simply using this as an excuse to go after these determined students and everything that they've achieved so far.

As The Justice Collective has proven to be effective in their ability to dismantle the red tape and bring actual damage to the immoral enforcers of the law, as they tend to call the police. A bunch of minors being able to push the needle so far, that they're being held illegally against their will with no parental oversight whatsoever.

Stuck inside a school building on a Saturday was already bad enough, but adding interrogation and intimidation tactics to that list simply made it that much worse. I sure hope we're able to make it before the cops are able to crack their spirit and demotivate them from their goal to improve the world for everyone in it.

NO JUSTICE
NO PEACE
BLM

CHAPTER 5:

To Lose A
Part Of You.

Narrator: Shaniece Davis

"Hold fast to dreams, for if
dreams die, life is a broken
winged bird that cannot fly."

Langston Hughes

5.1 THE BLACK GIRL EXPERIENCE

It was a 15 minute car ride to get to Deacon Valley High. In that short amount of time, I developed a very strong sense of connection to Shaniece. Even though I've only seen her through my phone screen, I could feel it.

Because in the past I used to be treated just like her, too young to be taken seriously, too Black to matter and too girly to hold a position of power. Just like me, Shaniece will grow up to be a woman stuck in a world built by men to forever hold on to their controlling privilege. Hated by everyone, from White to non-Black all the way to those living in her own African-American community.

Never was there a space for us to truly feel safe, protected and supported to become the best possible version of ourselves. Rather than a doormat destined to serve while expecting to sacrifice all of our hopes, dreams and aspirations because everyone expects us to. I truly look up to this girl, because she possesses a confidence that I could only dream of at her age. Determined to change her fate in the present by fighting for a better future, it makes me feel a sense of empowerment that I've never felt before.

I truly hope she's okay, and if not I'm pretty sure her father will raise hell to anyone who dared harm his little girl. Given his infamous reputation as a successful defense attorney I'm sure he'll be able to get her out safely. The main thing on my mind is trying to figure out why they're being held against their will, surely there has to be a greater scheme at play here. I can already smell the manipulation from afar, something bigger is going on here and I have a feeling I'm about to find out what it is.

Upon arrival at the school's parking lot, there were no cars around, only a school bus that was still fully decorated from yesterday's graduation ceremony. Shaniece did mention in her livestream that every member of The Justice Collective was collected and transported to school for further questioning. Apparently they wanted to stage a protest during the ceremony, but Principal Tanner was one step ahead of them so she was able to cancel it before it even had the chance to begin.

I guess Deacon Valley's police department wants to nip this in the bud as soon as possible. So that they can cut off the root of this rebellious tree before it than continue to grow in every state during the college experience.

If you think about it, it really is sad how a group of young teenagers are able to create so much panic and distress to every citizen in the valley. Simply by believing in themselves and their self-worth while actively fighting to break any glass ceiling that holds one of them down.

No matter how many years of so called progress pass by, the fight for justice and equality is one that will sadly never end. No matter how much change is implemented, a new system of injustice will work its way to the top yet again. But even though perfection is impossible to achieve, it can never hurt to aim for the next best thing.

That's what The Justice Collective is trying to do, making sure that the history of this country is never forgotten. By implementing change in their neighborhood without trying to wash away the regretful sins of the past.

5.3 HERE COMES THE REPORTER

Just as we were about to enter the school building, another car pulled up to the parking lot, it was a suspicious black van with tinted windows and 'T. J. C.' written in a large, bold white font. Apparently The Justice Collective has enough resources to demand their own personal form of transportation with an acronym representing their brand. I finally understand why the cops want to shut them down, as their influence was beyond measure. Making it impossible to calculate the damages to the unjust social construct of this timeless fake empire.

When the van finally parked, two people stepped out, one of them was Kiara Michaels, a social & moral justice reporter with a strong influence in the online realm. I've been following her posts for years now, but what the hell was she doing in this valley? Was she the one who sponsored them all and was she here to set the kids free?

The other was a younger man who resembled her very much, I can only guess that he's related to her somehow. He opened the van from the back and pulled out his camera equipment, he must be here to record the confrontation as Kiara never enters a situation without preparing for every possible outcome first. Which is very on brand for the woman who launched the meme that broke the internet. "Be ready! Look ready! Stay ready!"

When the young man turned his head towards us, he instantly froze, same for Darius who looked at him with his mouth wide open. So they have to know each other somehow, why does it feel like I'm starting to get entangled in a web that's impossible to escape from?

Both men just stood there in their tracks, I was trying to bring Darius back to earth while Kiara did the same for her... brother? Cousin? Counterpart? Whatever he's supposed to be to her, I don't know yet. First we had to get both of them back, I kept asking Darius what's wrong and all I heard were crickets. He just kept staring at the man while he did the same to Darius, and then he finally responded while Kiara & her counterpart approached us.

"That's Kieran, Deshawn's best friend who's already in college and the creator of The Justice Collective.

Even as a young adult he hasn't changed a bit, just as tall, dark and mysterious as his younger self, ...

Apparently we're not the only ones determined to free Shaniece and the rest of the collective.

This could probably turn out to be a very good thing, if he doesn't hate me for my regretful past of course."

When they stood face to face from us, Kieran offered up his hand and Darius didn't hesitate to shake it, I guess he understood that there was a bigger picture at play here.

Kieran the O.G. activist, Kiara the famous viral reporter, and Darius the successful defense attorney teaming up to save a group of rebellious students. I'm pretty sure Principal Tanner and the officers involved will deeply regret holding the students hostage without any form of parental consent. How could they not considering the power of resistance that's about to face them.

5.5 SAVED BY THE MEMORY SPELL

Before we entered we discussed about the best strategy to approach this tricky situation. Should we march in guns blazing, or yell out for them to come outside? There were so many strategies to choose from, but given the fact that Shaniece exposed this situation, it seemed only natural that Kiara Michaels would take the lead.

But just as we were about to walk inside, all of the students walked outside peacefully, walking in front of everyone were Shaniece and Principal Tanner. A woman in a full suit carrying a vibe with her that exudes a colonial energy that can only be described as White Feminism +.

It's like they were already prepared for us, in the back I could see the two police officers in uniform. As the group of students were all outside now they stopped moving while the officers approached. The first face I saw was an unfamiliar one who walked right past me on his way to the parking lot. Probably so he can start up the school bus and drive it closer to the entrance so the students can go back home. There was something about the way that he walked that just screamed dirty cop to me but I didn't make much of it at the time.

The second face was the one that floored me, it was Dylan Maxwell. I held it together to the best of my ability but I was dying inside. He gave me a weird look for a second, almost as if he saw me before. But luckily, Madame Davina's mindwipe proved to be effective. He turned his head back and stood next to the principle who was being berated by Kieran & Kiara, they were demanding an explanation for the mess that happened.

"There's no need to start filming this encounter as the situation has already been handled.

I personally called every single parent to let them know about our intentions today.

They were all eager to comply if it meant that yesterday's attempt to protest would remain buried.

So it wouldn't appear on their personal records as these students have yet to start their great college journey.

Everyone is free to leave, even the leader Shaniece, since we've already gotten what we came for.

Good luck trying to make us appear as the bad guys on your virtual platforms this time around."

I can't explain to you how much I already hate Principal Tanner, I've only met her once yet it feels like I've known her all my life. It's like her personality is a mix of every single abusive authority figure that I've come across. So suspicious and manipulative, as if there's no end that can't be justified by her oppressive means. She really thinks that she did something here, besides making The Justice Collective look like the victim to the public.

When I looked at the students they all seemed distraught and defeated, as if they no longer wanted to fight. Except for Shaniece, she looked too calm and collected, it almost seems like she's letting her think that the war is over, only to surprise her with a sudden final battle.

5.7 THE MOURNING OF A TWIN

Kieran & Kiara were not ready for Principal Tanner's deviously scheming ways, neither was Darius. She knew that she could use the natural worries of the parents to her advantage. Using subtle threats of an administrative nature to make the adults consent after the fact. What on earth is wrong with this woman for putting these kids through such mistreatment from the officers?

Was this her way of getting back at them for the years that she spent fighting off their demands for progression and reform? Was she really that salty and bitter to stoop so low as an adult to engage in a fight with children? Whatever her intentions were, it clearly did deliver some serious damage to the students and their very fragile and low level of self-esteem.

But Shaniece didn't give in, she just kept staring with a scheming look that radiated from her face. It seemed very sketchy to me so I got closer to her to find out more. But before I could even begin to introduce myself she already cut me off to say her peace.

"There's no need to introduce yourself, I know who you are because Deshawn told me in a dream. He told me you would be a valuable asset in our greatest struggle.

We've been expecting you for days now, for a moment it almost seemed like you would bail on us.

I assume you already heard about the seance that we need to perform so my brother can pierce through the veil long enough to tell us the real story?"

Shaniece explained everything to us, ever since Deshawn's death after the Juneteenth party, people have been seeing one-dimensional versions of his multi-dimensional character. Each version holding a different piece of his hopelessly broken soul, unable to be at rest until his dark truth can finally be revealed to the world.

What I saw as a mysterious figure, Darius saw as a violent poltergeist, while Shaniece has been having conversations with her brother underwater. As Deshawn would have graduated as captain of the swimming team had he not been killed in what seems to be a highly 'suspicious' tragedy. I would bet everything I have that Dylan is involved somehow. How could he not be given the fact that he was responsible for the paperwork of this case?

Deshawn told her that this would happen, she was already prepared for it, he even gave her the tip to outsmart Dylan by using his alpha male presence against him with the classic excuse of period problems. She was already prepared with a red nail polish tampon, as her cycle had already passed earlier in the month of June.

Apparently, Deshawn had also told her about the seance, and that it shouldn't be today but rather tomorrow. As a new tragedy was about to unfold that would take away most of our time today, she had no idea what it was, neither did her spirit brother. All he could tell her was that it would make life a living hell for all of us, leaving no one spared. And just like that, a sudden explosive blast made all of us drop to the ground in a panicked frenzy that could only be induced by excessive levels of fear.

5.9 THE SOUND OF A BLAST

No one could have predicted that there was a bomb strapped to the school bus engine. It was the plot twist that raised the stakes to the highest possible level. Yet another officer of the law brutally killed in under 24 hours, this place was about to turn into a warzone that would most definitely cause more civilian casualties.

Now everyone will think that the killer is among us, how could they not when you take into account that we were the only ones present to commit such a crime. Even I'm starting to doubt whether or not these kids had something to do with this, so imagine how the average Jane & Joe would think about these suspicious circumstances.

Dylan immediately got back up and yelled out his partner's name, in such a high tone, we could all hear it loudly. Even though our ear drums were still numb from the piercingly loud sound of the explosive blast. "DEVIN! NOOOOOO!!!" He yelled out through the top of his lungs, it almost made me feel bad for him. Almost being the key word here, as this blood feud was clearly happening for a reason, meaning there must be some level of guilt there. As the smoke started to rise up in the air Dylan contacted his dispatch while Principal Tanner dialed 911 to alert the blast.

The only thing that remained somewhat intact was the graduation sash that was draped over the side of the bus. The ends slightly burnt off but the message was still very clear and easy to read for everyone

"Congratulations class of 2023!"

It took us all a moment to fully process what happened, most of the students broke down in tears. While Principal Tanner simply froze in absolute shock, her brain could not process what she experienced just now. While Kieran & Kiara looked neither sad nor happy, as if they didn't want this to happen, but also that they didn't care at all about the life of a cop being taken from the world.

Darius was looking absolutely panicked, since he already knows from experience that the police investigators will have a field day with this wacked out case. A group of mainly Black & Brown rebellious students caught up in a series of officer deaths where the killer wears a mask that was designed by the creator of The Justice Collective. Darius already knew that society would view every single one of them as an accomplice. While those who still dared to resist and fight back would immediately be branded with the permanent mark of the guilty.

I mean, I don't even need to investigate to know that The Beast Of Liberty was behind this. Based on his first video message it was clear that we have yet to experience the craziest elements of his highly destructive schemes. I'm sure of it and so is Dylan since he can't seem to stop staring at the wall facing the school bus.

He grabbed his cellphone & took a picture of the wall, this triggered all of us to move closer as well. Upon arrival, we saw a Guy Fawkes mask in a T.J.C. style painted in graffiti, with a quote in a bloody red color.

"Love your rage, not your cage!"

NO JUSTICE
NO PEACE
BLM

CHAPTER 6:

To Organize A Viral Protest.

Narrator: Kieran Michaels

"In the end Anti-Black, Anti-Female & all forms of discrimination are equivalent to the same thing: Anti-Humanism."

Shirley Chisholm

6.1 CANCELED BY THE RULE OF LAW

We were all taken to the Deacon Valley police station for questioning, they kept us there for hours without letting us know when we would be free to leave. There was no way they could pin this on us, but that was not their intention. The cops simply wanted to make us look guilty in the eyes of the public, making their reasoning for the interrogation seem valid due to this explosive tragedy.

Every police officer that passed by gave us the look of death, as if they wanted to find an excuse to pull their trigger, except for the officers of color. Their sense of grief seemed staged in my eyes, I guess that should tell me enough about the type of police officer that Devin Rogers was and what kind of impact his death will have.

I truly feel for these kids, they worked so hard for years to define and anker their brand, simply to have that identity perverted in the name of vigilante justice. Everyone will treat them differently now, some may even have their college scholarships revoked given the severity of this investigation. Will this murder spree become the most violent series of cop killings in our country's history?

If The Beast Of Liberty has something to say about it, then it most certainly will be the case. He has everyone shook and every cop in the valley marches to the beat of this psychotic vigilante's drum. How many more deaths will follow? Surely his diabolical plan isn't as simple as weeding out all of the dirty seeds that ruin the name and integrity of Deacon Valley P.D.? If so, then we may truly have a widescale bloodbath coming up, with consequences so dire for innocent bystanders.

By the time we were released, the bright sunny sky from before had already turned into a sultry summer evening. We were all still in shock, completely drained mentally and physically due to everything that's happened today. No matter how hard The Justice Collective tries to process the events that occurred today, the main consensus was that the battle for the cause ended in a defeat that may have permanent consequences for public perception. They were truly broken and seeing that burned out look in their eyes crushed both my heart and my soul.

Every single parent, even aunt Jasmine stood outside the entrance of the police department, waiting to embrace their children. The students were so tired of their unfortunate realities that they didn't even make a fuss. They simply no longer cared to fight, not even to confront their parents for giving their consent for the original interrogation. They just walked outside with no sense of pride nor victory, as if they tried to take on the weight of world & deeply suffered as a result of it.

Even Shaniece was crying her eyes out as she crashed on her mother's shoulder. Unable to cope with the endless paranoia that occurs as a direct result of feeling like you're never seen, accepted nor loved by your fellow humans. To feel such a strong sense of self-loathing at such a young age, and having to grow up like that with no true escape, it can do some very serious damage to derail your journey towards becoming a healthy adult. I can confirm that theory based on my experience into adulthood, and knowing Kiara's journey that she shared with the internet she knows exactly what I'm talking about as well.

6.3 NEVER BACKING DOWN

As every member of the collective was sobbing beyond measure, O.G. Kieran couldn't stand to see the sight of such a hopeless sense of loss. So he rallied all of them together to make sure they didn't lose the will to keep on fighting and resisting the systems of oppression that to this day still hold control of the world. If The Justice Collective was a cheerleading team then surely the inspiring creator Kieran Michaels would forever be known in history as its timeless all-star cheer captain.

Since he didn't need more than a few minutes to lift their moods and inspire them with a new burning sense of activism. They no longer saw themselves as mere victims of an unjust society, but rather as fierce warriors on a mission to better the world.

This young man exudes such a powerful form of confidence that affects everyone in his surroundings. It truly is no wonder that he created this movement and why he holds such a strong influence on its members even two years after he graduated. He even came up with a motto that's basically a revised phrase from the story that inspired the creation of their masked branding. Kieran made every member stand next to each other to form a united line, and they continued to chant this motto while they marched to the cops at the entrance.

"Remember, remember the 26th of February where a Black one was killed with the offensive firing of a shot!

For 10 years later still no one has found a way to change the system so that our lives are no longer left to rot!"

The impact of that cry for resistance was impossible to describe with mere words, you had to be there to feel its effects. It felt so damn empowering to watch the officers stare out of their windows in absolute discomfort. How could they not considering the fact that one motivational speech undid all of the damage they had caused today.

To make matters even worse for them, all of this adversity simply made the hunger for change and desire for resistance grow exponentially among the members of The Justice Collective. They were all reborn from the ashes of their previous failure, screaming at the top of their lungs so that their voices were loud & clear. This time around, no one would silence them, as that has been done more than enough already.

Some parents took this magnificent moment to social media and within a few minutes this revolt went viral. The footage being shared all across the country, probably awakening a whole new wave of civil protests that will surely spread all across the globe. It never ceases to amaze me how fast things go these days. One minute you're streaming something and the next the whole world is watching the entire event unfold step by step.

And yet another benefit to immediately going viral was that mainstream journalists were nowhere to be seen. Giving Kiara ample opportunity to go around creating a news segment of her own. Where everything is defined based on her vision as a reporter. Rather than the network's vision of a manipulated vessel who stands in front of a camera as a robot forever stuck on a mission.

6.5 PROTEST IN THE NAME OF JUSTICE

After a while Kieran and Kiara joined together to calm down the students. Since they had communicated their message loud and clear so now the time had come to step down and regroup at a later time. As everyone started to walk back to their car, only Dylan stormed outside of the precinct, alongside of him a highly intimidating authority figure walked at a similarly aggressive pace.

I could only think that he was the big man in charge, his age and the way he walked towards us confirmed it. He gave me a heavy colonizer energy, it was so visible that it made my spirit feel infected with a toxic masculinity carrying virus. But the real kicker came when he got close enough for me to read his nametag; Nicholas Tanner! Could it be that he's the principal's husband?

If so, then I must say they were meant to be as they matched each other perfectly on a visual level. Both of them presenting as authority figures who need to control every single element of their immediate surroundings. If even the slightest form of chaos was visible, they would spontaneously combust.

And my assumptions were correct as Madeline Tanner instantly walked towards her husband to embrace him. Her frightened soul causing her entire body to shiver, making her husband uneasy in the process. All while both he and Dylan looked at us with such contempt.

It was almost as if they wanted nothing more than to shoot all of us on sight, like they wouldn't even bat an eyelash & sleep like babies after assassinating us...

That deadly stare couldn't have been longer than a minute but it seemed like time stood still yet again. While an intense series of cold shivers made us all feel so uncomfortable, as if we were neither wanted nor safe in their environment. To be fair, I don't even think any of us would ever want any type of connection to them anyway so it's not like we're missing out on anything fun.

It's just the way they looked at us that really shook me, it made me realize that this was the way that we were always looked at from the very beginning of our presence in this country. No matter how many insincere forms of societal progress add another filter to make this look seem less hostile. Once a certain situation gets too real it always reverts back to that original sense of hostility.

It's an intense look that tells you so much without using any actual words. It reminds you that you're never truly welcome no matter how hard you try to fit in. While confirming that they will always try to keep us down so they can continue to uphold their claim over us. Because if they didn't then they would have to stop appropriating our world. Which means they have to actively start working on their perception of us and that they no longer hold a claim to what we say, do, and want in the world..

I'm pretty sure that they would all rather let hell freeze over before they would allow us to gain even the slightest form of autonomy. Even the ones that actually want to see us do good, would feel some type of way if they ever saw us doing better than them. That's just the reality of our experience as Black people in the United States.

6.7 WHEN THE TEA STARTS TO SPILL

After the hostile look of death, Dylan and the Tanners turned and walked back to the precinct. While we all continued to walk to the parking lot. Everyone left and it was just me and the Davis/Michaels crews that were still there, our cars were all still parked at school. While aunt Jasmine could only fit four people in her vehicle.

She suggested that I take a cab while she brought home Shaniece, and much to his surprise Darius was also invited to spend the night at their house. Shaniece also urged Kiara to join them, she had something that she needed to show her back at the house. Kiara agreed and asked Kieran to join me on the cab ride to the motel.

And just as we're about to get ready to say goodbye we all receive a viral text blast. Looks like The Beast Of Liberty channeled his inner Riddler for this one.

"I have countless bruises from police brutality, and yet none of them were officially reported.

I have seen law enforcement commit countless other atrocities against our people, and yet none of them were exposed to the masses by mainstream media.

I have yet to show my face, but the mask I carry already threatens to disrupt Deacon Valley's societal order.

What or better yet who am I???

By the end of tomorrow all of you will find out,
but for tonight I'll just expose dear old Devin..."

The message had us staring at our screens with a wide open mouth and a mind lost in all possible forms of translation. No one knows what kind of game he's playing, everyone simply serves as a pawn that he can steer with little to no difficulty whatsoever. By the time his killing spree comes to an end, The Beast Of Liberty will have changed every aspect of the societal game.

There's no doubt about is that he's a catalyst, and based on the strained communication happening in front of my eyes due to his riddle, it's more than clear to me now what kind of game he's playing. He's pitting two different worlds against each other so that they can collide and let God decide the victor of this timeless battle.

The first world being governed by the steady power of tradition, where anchors that have existed throughout the realms of time should continue to exist even if they developed severely problematic elements over the years. This was clearly visible in the way that aunt Jasmine and Darius clapped back at Kieran, Kiara and Shaniece.

Which immediately brings us to the second world, governed by the variable power of revolution. Where sacrificing the past and its problematic aspects are an absolute requirement to bring a permanent form of change in the world. This mentality almost seems deeply rooted in the collective tapestry of any young one's soul.

Two completely different worlds headed towards a Clash Of Titans, when they should be finding a way to band together as that will make them stronger in the end.

6.9 OFFICER DEVIN ROGERS EXPOSED

After a short amount of bickering, everyone managed to calm down rather easily. Most likely they were all just too tired after experiencing a day of absolute hell, I know I was. There were simply too many variables in today's equation, I'm not sure how I'm still standing here.

If this were any other paranormal investigation I would've been long gone while proudly taking the L. But the blood connection has me bound until my work here is done. Aunt Jasmine drove off with the others while Kieran and I waited only a few minutes for an Uber driver to arrive at the police department.

Once inside, I could tell Kieran was struggling with something, so when I tried to ask what was wrong he nodded his head towards the driver, his presence made him too uncomfortable so I let it go, for now...

I turned my head to the window and lovingly stared at the evening sky, basking in all of its sultry glory. It was the only actual moment of piece that I was able to experience today. Until it was interrupted by yet another viral blast, just like clockwork The Beast Of Liberty makes good on his promise. Every single case that lead to the filing of a complaint against Devin was leaked online.

An endless series of complaints relating to racism, misogyny and corruption, basically the colonial White man's ultimate trifecta. I was rather shocked to see the amount of complaints, especially since none of them managed to get on his permanent record. I guess it pays off to be graced with so much privilege in the world.

When we arrived at the motel, it was almost as if a higher power wanted to push us to continue our chat since the lobby was closed. Apparently Nora was busy running yet another 'errand', as she tends to do often.

So that meant dear old Kieran was trapped, with nowhere to go as he hopelessly looked around for the world's sketchiest motel keeper. But she was still nowhere to be found so he caved rather quickly.

I didn't even have to pry anything out of him, all I did was ask him what was on his mind & he replied swiftly.

"There was a time when Deandre Fredricks was a kind-hearted kid, he was our friend and both Deshawn and I were closer to him than we were to each other.

Until he saw his father Jacob get killed when the cops invaded the wrong house in a drug bust gone bad.

Ever since then, he completely snapped and despised every officer in sight, always creating riddles & clues to suggest that he was plotting their permanent downfall.

All day long I thought The Beast Of Liberty was on a mission to destroy the police department in general.

But that message and these clues, they're alarmingly on brand for the way that Deandre used to share a message.

The beast has to be connected to him specifically, I just have no idea how and no way of finding out either..."

NO JUSTICE
NO PEACE
BLM

CHAPTER 7:

To Be A Queen Of Nubia.

Narrator: Kiara Michaels

"Think like a queen. A queen is not afraid to fail. Failure is another steppingstone to greatness."

Oprah Winfrey

7.1 STILL NOWHERE TO BE FOUND

It was like Nora was not planning on returning to the motel tonight. The longer she stayed absent, the more Kieran began to spiral. He was ranting and speculating, never staying still in just one place, but moving around so much that it was starting to make me feel dizzy.

He was bringing up every single experience he had with Deandre, hoping it would bring us clues. But all it really did was depress the both of us to a point of no return. But still Kieran tried to speculate until his body got the shivers, this must mean my mother has another clue. He eventually stopped shaking, looked me dead in the eyes and delivered a truly disturbing message from mother.

"Ma Chérie, I fear that the plans for tomorrow's
séance have changed.

For the spirits of this valley have alerted me that
a different strategy will be applied.

One that will result in a river of martyred blood,
that brings with it a massive, rebellious flood.

I know you feel connected with your bloodline, but
please leave this place as soon as possible!

This is the last time you will hear from me again, as
the ancestors have requested my presence."

Just as Kieran snapped back into his own mind and acted like nothing had happened. Kiara pulled up in her van, immediately jumped out and began to ramble.

THE SPIRITS OF ANCIENT NUBIA 7.2

Kiara was so jumpy, it was like she had witnessed something from beyond the veil of perception. She kept talking about the ancestral spirits and their magical plan to change the reality of our world. Kieran eventually managed to hold her down until she started to relax.

After a brief questioning we found out that Kiara accompanied Shaniece on one of her visits to the other side. Where they were able to visit a fragment of his martyred soul, they buried their heads in a bucket full of water and met with him in a dreamscape that resembled Deacon Valley's famous Trinity square.

Where the three main churches stood together on one line, the Black church on the left side, Hispanic church on the right and the White church stuck in the middle. Deshawn apparently warned them that The Beast Of Liberty was only beginning his rampage and that way more bloodshed would take place in this soon to be Thunderdome. He urged his sister to stay safe while also reminding her that sometimes it was better to die on your feet rather than to live on your knees.

Then he spoke of the ancestors whose spirits have suffered for centuries witnessing their descendants go through so much oppression. But they have had it and are going to set the necessary pawns in motion. For now, Kiara was simply instructed by him to go visit Deandre's mother Tasha Fredricks. Kiara had no idea why she had to but suspected something was up when she saw Kieran instantly turn his head towards me with a shocked facial expression that screams out paranoia.

7.3 A GIRL POWER EXPEDITION

Shaniece clearly stated that I had to join Kiara on this mission, she never mentioned Kieran so he had the option to join if he wanted to. But his anxious facial expression and shaky posture was a clear sign that he had no intention of joining us to Creeper's Corner.

He preferred to wait for Nora to arrive so he could get a 2-person room, even if he had to wait in the parking lot alone. Kiara wouldn't have it and a clash of siblings erupted right in front of my eyes. I couldn't even begin to interject as both sides were coming for each other with absolutely no chance of a ceasefire to take place.

I couldn't take it anymore and walked forward to place myself in the middle. Hoping it would distract them so they can focus their attention on me, and I was right. They stopped bickering and looked at me expecting something to happen, so I pulled out my room key and gave it to Kieran. I told him it was protected by my late mother's sorcerous charms which seemed to calm the both of them down. Kieran took the key and seemed less anxious all of a sudden, he gracefully bowed his head to show his appreciation towards me.

Kiara then walked up to him and they hugged out their issues, as if nothing ever happened. They were just so pressed on keeping each other safe, understandable since they grew up as orphans in a valley that made them feel nothing but an invisible sense of self-hatred. I patiently waited as they continued to embrace, then Kiara turned and signaled me to get inside the van and we drove off while Kieran waved us off from the stairs.

It was a very silent car ride at first, we were both too uncomfortable to hold a conversation with one another. Even though I've been following her online journey for years, it's different when you interact with someone live. After a while, Kiara grew tired of it and asked me what was on my mind. I took a deep breath and asked her why she came back to Deacon Valley to which she replied:

"I had a dream about a beautiful curly haired woman in a bright red dress playing with her son.

She let me play along and told me that my home-town would be expecting my arrival very soon.

Before I could even ask her why, I woke up from my slumber and saw my feeds going crazy with posts of the Maxwells getting killed by The Beast Of Liberty."

I was visibly shocked by her answer and she immediately noticed something was wrong. I tried to deflect her but yet again she managed to beat around the bush. While simultaneously tricking me to give her the answers to the questions that she wanted to hear. I eventually gave in & let her know that I had the same dream at the same time.

At first she looked at me with a skeptical look, but then as I explained the three phases of my dream she shared my visibly shocked facial expression. Apparently, that was exactly how it went for her as well, she just told me a beautified version of the truth. This has to mean that we're connected somehow, it just has to! We just have no idea how this bond works and how deep it truly goes...

7.5 A DISTRICT OF RED LIGHTS

When you go beyond the motel's reach that is where you'll find the beacon of red lights. Where payment is required for any type of sexual service. No matter how freaky your intentions, you will always find someone willing to engage in it if the price is right. Only normal that it's located such a short drive from the motel from a business point of view. So the people wouldn't have to risk getting caught by someone.

If this wasn't graduation weekend then I'm sure that Nora would be working triple shifts to clean all the rooms in time to accommodate the next customers. But there was no way to fit in this type of fun in their extremely busy schedule of their children's graduation ceremonies. So the red lights workers have a weekend holiday much to their chagrin.

There were so many woman there, of all ethnicities and colors, desperately waiting for a stream of income to arrive. They were so eager for a client that even we were getting offers left right and center from the moment we arrived. I was hurt to see so many women doing something that in my heart I know most of them didn't willingly choose. As many don't have the luxury of being given a choice from multiple options. But rather are conditioned to do whatever it takes to put food on the table, even if most of them hated every second of the act that they were instructed to perform.

They simply did it, and put some of the money they received into drugs that were then used to shoot up and be numb enough to no longer feel the trauma.

THE FREDRICKS MATRIARCH 7.6

It didn't take us long to find Tasha Fredricks, since she's the veteran matriarch of Creeper's Corner. She created the district along with her husband Jacob, long before Deandre was born. When her dear husband died in a drug raid which was alerted to the authorities on a bogus call. Tasha left behind her son with the in-laws and made Creeper's Corner her new home. Building it further to include more than just heterosexual desires.

You could tell by her wrinkled face and wrecked body that this woman has been through a lot. Growing up in a broken home with no true sense of love nor safety can do that to a person, the same probably goes for all of the workers here. Would all of them truly choose this life as an adult, if they were given better options as a child? Either way, at least Tasha takes care of them as long as they can pay their commission.

When she saw us step out of the van, her first reaction was very positive, she stared and complimented both of us on our black beauty. It soon became clear that she thought we were applying to work for her, but Kiara diffused that situation rather swiftly. It was then that Tasha remembered who she was. Which was a shock for Kiara who thought she forgot all about her due to the narcotics that flooded her system while permanently infecting her hopelessly broken mind.

Then she found out that we were here for intel on her boy Deandre and her eyes instantly teared up. she looked away and gave us the signal to leave. But Kiara yet again stood firm in her conviction until Tasha finally cracked.

7.7 AN INTERACTION WITH THE BEAST

"I can't tell you what happened to my boy Deandre.

I only remember seeing him with Old Man Ray at the Juneteenth celebration party.

They were about to ugh..."

And then a sudden loud bang made Kiara and I widen our eyes to a maximum with a mouth just as wide open and blood spatters all over our faces. Tasha Fredricks, suddenly taken from her life by one swift and highly accurate headshot. Her head damn near exploded as the rest of her body crashed straight to the ground.

Then we heard footsteps approaching but we were both completely frozen in our tracks. Unable to move while our breathing was so heavy it seemed like we were both in a hospital room delivering a baby. He kept moving closer to us, while our hearts kept beating faster and faster, our bodies still unable to move from a pure sense of paralyzing shock.

And then, he stood in front of us, for the first time we were able to see him in person, instead of the video messages that he left behind. The Beast Of Liberty in the flesh! If people thought his presence was scary on screen then the live performance would bring most individuals a heart attack. Kiara & I turned our heads towards each other, both of us displaying a facial expression of absolute terror. Our lips trembling while the tears running from our eyes started to mix with the many drops of blood that were already covering our melanated faces.

We just stood there completely distraught as the workers in the background screamed in panic. Not only did they lose their matriarch at that moment, they also became exposed to every single third party who felt scorned that their partners needed to seek out their services.

They lost the one person who protected them like only a mother could do, and now they could be the next victim just like we could be. The Beast Of Liberty walked towards Tasha's lifeless body, put his hands around her neck and yanked off the chain she wore with her son's initials draped in a solid gold execution. He put the chain in his pocket and marched towards us.

He walked closer until we stood face to face towards each other, while Kiara stared in absolute panic as she worried about my well-being. But to our surprise he lowered his gun, giving off the idea that we wouldn't be harmed. He reached out his hand and aimed his finger to point towards my purse & I gave it to him with no hesitation whatsoever. He slowly opened it and then came the shock that made my heart sink to my stomach. He knew exactly where I was hiding the note that made Dylan Maxwell seek me out last night and threaten me at gunpoint.

I safely put it in a hidden zipper in the bottom right corner, he didn't look around and instantly grabbed it. He put the note in his pocket and pulled out his gun again giving us the signal to immediately drive away. As much as I wanted to stay and get back my safety, I certainly wanted to run for my life that much more.

7.9 THE WILDEST NIGHT RIDE

Neither of us had said a word to each other the entire ride back to the motel. I kept looking outside of my passenger window. While Kiara's eyes were firmly planted on the road, it was almost like she was expecting another surprise to come through.

Surely, The Beast Of Liberty wouldn't have followed us as it made no sense to do so. And even if he did, I honestly couldn't care at this point. Since the note that protected me from Dylan Maxwell was no longer in my possession, I'm more worried about him and what he could do when his memories start coming back.

The only thing truly on my mind right now was how we could survive this mess. Not even the fact that Tasha's head damn near exploded from that close-up headshot phased me enough to distract me of the constant state of panic that my mind was stuck in.

I tried my best to hide it, but was no match for Kiara as her snoopy reporter instincts were always on point. She was just about to ask if I was okay until she got a text message that made her gasp as she immediately stepped on the gas to accelerate. When I asked her why she was speeding up she showed me her phone, apparently her brother Kieran sent her an urgent message.

"Sis, I have a feeling something's wrong, I can sense it, I feel like my life is in danger right now.

If something happens to me, please know that I love you with all of my heart, always and forever."

For the very first time in her adult life, the flawless Kiara Michaels found herself unable to bring up her guard as she was too busy oozing out emotional vulnerability. It was weird seeing her like this, as if I thought her poker inspired game face was actually her natural composure.

But it turned out I was very wrong, the way she stepped on the gas as every bone in her body was shaking aggressively made me notice that her image was just a shell. Built to give off the impression that her skin was made of the thickest possible materials. When in reality it was just as fragile and flawed as the skin of any other human being that tries to live their best possible life.

She was so stuck on getting to her brother that she didn't even think to ask me about the note that was taken from me. Neither did I to be honest, since I was way too concerned for both her well-being as that of Kieran's. Since he didn't strike me as the type of person to send a message like that as a mere joke.

There was definitely something going on and as we pulled up to the motel our instincts turned out to be truthful. We were blinded by the police siren lights on the one hand, and flashing camera lights on the other. The motel parking lot was full of reporters and officers as tragedy had just unfolded. When Kiara parked her van and stepped outside, the reporters swarmed around her the same way that moths tend to do when they gather around a flame. I was too anxious to get out and just witnessed it from my window. Even like this I could still feel her pain when she saw him on that stretcher.

NO JUSTICE
NO PEACE
BLM

CHAPTER 8:

To Feel A
Mom's Wrath.

Narrator: Katie Maxwell

"In a racist society, it is not
enough to be non-racist.
We must be anti-racist."

Angela Davis

8.1 THE FURIOUS CASE OF PROFILING

Apparently, Nora had arrived at the motel not long after we left for Creeper's Corner. When she saw Kieran, a tall, dark-skinned black man she felt 'threatened'. My god how I have grown to hate that word, since it's been used to hold us all back for so long. She called 911 to alert the authorities, and Dylan Maxwell gladly agreed to follow up on it, probably since his memories had no longer been wiped clean. But it truly is suspicious how quickly he arrived at the scene, could it be that he was already trailing us since our visit to the precinct?

Poor Kieran didn't even stand a chance, no wonder he sent his sister a panicked message, it was the only thing he could do at the time. While the reporters were throwing jabs at her in the form of some very conniving questioning, Kiara stepped away from them so she could see the ambulance leave with her brother fighting for his life.

She then stepped towards Dylan, as if she was really ready to do something, at that point I decided to step out of the van and hold her down so I could keep her safe. All the while she kept screaming and hurling insults at Dylan who seemed to keep his game face under control. While police chief Tanner stood next to him, also berating him since there's no way they could possibly spin this on Kieran, no cover-up could ever work!

He was unarmed and was given the key to my room voluntarily, so no official laws had been violated. Therefore it made no sense to shoot first and ask questions later, especially since there were no signs of resistance. Even Nora seemed genuinely regretful of her blunt actions.

Poor Kiara was totally spiraling in my arms, in so much suffering emotionally that it actually brought her physical pain. I was too focused on helping her calm down that I completely forgot about Dylan and how he would react to seeing me. When our eyes connected it truly felt like he was fighting the urge not to pull out his gun again to pull the trigger. It wasn't just me who noticed it as Kiara seemed suspicious of his reaction towards me, I felt unsafe so all that I could think of was getting out of there.

But there was no way we could escape both the reporters blocking the van, and psycho Dylan with his posse who were blocking the steps to my motel room since it was now a crime scene. We were stuck in an exposed state of adversity and everyone around us lived for this moment in which our sense of pain equaled their sense of satisfaction. As they branded us nothing more than objects of absolute victimhood identified by nothing but an essence of endless suffering. In this highly devastating moment, my heart truly went out to Kiara as she buried her head deep inside my neck to escape all the attention.

And here we go yet again, just when all hope for a safe escape seems completely lost, a new surprise comes to the rescue. Since Darius arrived at the motel, immediately jumping out and violently pushing his way past the reporters to check on our well-being. It was the first time in my life that I didn't mind being a damsel in distress that required saving from a basic man with a hero complex. After he knew that we were ok, he distracted everyone by pointing all eyes towards him as he promised that this tragedy would have some severe legal consequences.

8.3 A SUDDEN RACE TO THE HOSPITAL

Both the media and law enforcement were completely taken aback by Darius. Who basically attacked them with his aggressive and highly intimidating legal strategy. No one even looked at the two of us anymore. We were now just background fillers, mere victims of a system that was designed to forever keep us down as our equality was an immediate threat to their privileged superiority. But at least we were able to escape that wretched scene and speed our way to the hospital so Kiara could be with her brother who was still fighting for his life. The both of us owe Darius for that at the very least, even though he clearly took personal pleasure in being the savior that threatened to crush the current power establishment.

I was driving this time around, since Kiara was just way too upset to do so, stuck in her own mind as she played out every single possible doom scenario in her head. I had never driven as fast in my entire life, but even that was too slow for her, she just kept urging me to step on the gas even more. She wanted to be there to keep her younger brother safe, as not only was his life at risk so was his right to be treated as an equal in this society.

For a man of his complexion that gets shot by a police officer is immediately branded as a bad individual who simply had it coming. No matter what the circumstances were of the shooting, they would find something about him that could be spun into a reasoning that validated his unworthiness of possible innocence until proven guilty. Even the medics responsible for his survival would find themselves questioning his character before any reliable facts were presented to them.

THE WAITING ROOM ASSEMBLY 8.4

We were the first to arrive, much to Kieran's luck head nurse Joy was on call tonight, an older woman who very much resembled Lisa Maxwell. She had the same fair skin with silver-gray hair and a beautifully disarming smile that can warm up even the coldest of hearts. She immediately recognized Kiara who started crying when she laid eyes on her, as if she wanted to be nursed. Joy stepped up to Kiara and they hugged each other in a way that only a mother and daughter could. I guess she's the mother figure who filled the parental void that was felt by both siblings in their orphaned childhood. She led us to the waiting room and brought us a warm, cup of tea.

The room was empty, it was only the two of us, Joy had left to continue her work and she promised to find out how Kieran was doing. Which gave Kiara a limited sense of peace as she hugged Joy once again, but without tears this time around. As time passed, Shaniece, aunt Jasmine and members of the collective accompanied by their parents started to arrive. All of them completely distraught by the tragic events that had taken place earlier tonight. Later on, teachers of Deacon Valley high joined in, all of them left with a truly unsettling feeling after seeing one of their former pupils go through something like this.

It was the first time that they had fully opened their eyes to the many causes that The Justice Collective actively tried to fight for. Which led to a conversation that everyone needed to hear. One where it was no longer about finding the perfect culprit for the existing problems. But rather about finding a way to finally keep the seemingly endless transgressions of human history in the past.

8.5 WHEN TWO MOTHERS COLLIDE

As the important conversations continued to flow, Kiara couldn't even be bothered to get involved. She kept staring at the door hoping to see head nurse Joy walk in and deliver some hopefully good news. Since this endlessly paranoid state of the unknown is dangerous enough to destabilize even the most balanced of minds. My brain was also stuck on Kieran's well-being, but not due to a bond established on the sibling principle. But rather because I had a really bad case of survivor's guilt.

Since Kieran got shot in the room that I let him enter, right while psycho Dylan was experiencing flashbacks to a recently wiped memory. Flashbacks so intense that it probably brought back all of that same angry energy that flowed through his vessel when he was putting my life in danger for the sake of undercover investigation. Since I was nowhere to be found at that moment, he took out that rage on the most adjacent vessel in his vicinity, consequences be damned. If he dies, then I'll truly never be able to forgive myself for coming here.

As we heard footsteps approaching, Kiara immediately ordered all of us to be quiet. Everyone was focused on the door, hoping it was Joy rather than someone else who had to wait on a loved one. When the door finally opened, it wasn't a nurse but a Caucasian woman with blond hair, blue eyes and a look on her face that simply screamed outrage. It was Katie Maxwell, the spouse of Dylan who looked like she was possessed by the spirit of the original Karen. Everyone was shocked to see her, it made aunt Jasmine so upset that she instantly rose up from her chair and charged towards Katie.

When I tell you that a lion destroying a gazelle seemed like a loving encounter compared to the beatdown that I just witnessed, I truly mean it. Aunt Jasmine did not hold back, she tackled Katie to the ground and started wailing on her left, right and center. The hits looked precise and anything but gentle, meaning that more than just one bruise was left behind on her face. If it was Halloween right now, Katie wouldn't even need any make-up nor a costume to come off as scary.

She just had to publicly engage in someone else's business to awaken an eerie zombie Karen vibe. Since it was clear that none of the parents nor the children cared for her safety. When I looked around, I even saw a few faces taking pleasure in her beatdown, especially Shaniece had a smile on her face that made me believe she was living for this moment. After a while, it simply became too much for me to handle so I decided to intervene and separate the two. I then held aunt Jasmine in my arms so she could cry out the rest of her pent up frustration.

It's very clear to me that what she wanted to do to Dylan earlier today, she projected onto his wife since he would also suffer from Katie's physical pain. I'm not a medic so I can't tell whether or not she needed medical attention. But an icepack surely seemed appropriate to reduce the swelling of all the bloody knots forming on her head.

Aunt Jasmine beat Katie down so badly that it brought damage to her own hands. All the while, Kiara still stared at the doorframe hoping for the news that liberates her from the scary and dark place of the unknown.

8.7 A SUSPICIOUS KARENISATION

Katie started bawling her eyes out, while she continued to lay on the floor, completely broken and bruised. We all simply stood there confused as to why she would show up here, especially now of all times. Since Kieran is still being operated on after her husband Dylan shot him twice. Eventually Shaniece approached Katie and asked her why she decided to come to the hospital. To which she responded while still in full ugly cry mode.

"I didn't come here to fight, I'm just looking for my daughter Hannah.

She's been missing all day, I've tried looking everywhere and I just can't reach her.

I thought she would be here with all of you."

Shaniece and everyone else seemed very confused by that answer, apparently they haven't seen or talked to Hannah ever since Deshawn's funeral. This answer seemed to Karenize Katie who then stopped crying and got back up with her signature crazy facial expression. She didn't believe them and kept throwing out accusations that made no sense whatsoever.

When Shaniece clapped back at her, Katie started going off even more, she just couldn't believe that Hannah did not try to contact them. When Shaniece asked her why the answer she gave made us all gasp.

"Because I know my daughter and your twin were lovers, so don't stand there and keep playing ignorant with me!"

This sudden reveal was one that no one knew anything about, Katie could clearly see that she was the only one who was aware of this. Apparently, the two of them had been dating since the summer, even before their senior year had begun. But Katie only found out from Hannah herself after Deshawn's untimely demise two weeks ago.

The news made everyone go quiet, they loved Hannah so they didn't understand why she would keep this a secret. While Shaniece stood there in shock since she had no idea that her twin had a romantic situation going on that she knew absolutely nothing about.

Aunt Jasmine was also shocked to find out about this news, she had no idea her son was romantically involved with Katie's daughter. At first, she seemed rather skeptical but after that it all came together in her head as if she found the missing pieces of this dark puzzle.

She was just about to engage in a conversation when we suddenly heard footsteps approaching yet again. Was it head nurse Joy who would bring a real update on Kieran's situation? Or was it yet another unforeseen visit by a third party that doesn't belong here in this waiting room with us? The suspense was truly killing me as it seemed like the individual was walking ridiculously slow on purpose. Even Kiara was getting frustrated as she immediately closed her eyes and started squinting. As if she was praying to a higher power to bring her the news she so desperately needed to hear. The news of positivity that would make her happy to be alive rather than the news of negativity that would make her wish she was dead.

8.9 A NEAR-DEATH EXPERIENCE

It turned out to be nurse Joy who entered with a big smile on her face, she wasted no time and let us know that Kieran survived the critical surgery. The bullet that hit his shoulder was merely a flesh wound, but the one in the gut was a high risk that could've ended his life.

But they were able to remove the bullet, and now his condition has been stabilized. So he can expect a full recovery after a long journey of healing. Kiara was so relieved that she jumped in nurse Joy's arms. Completely breaking down while thanking Joy for doing what she could to bring her this positive message. You could feel that the mood within the waiting room had shifted from hopeless to hopeful. Since their role model had managed to survive a dangerous situation that most people who shared his Black experience wouldn't.

Even Katie seemed genuinely relieved, but it was probably because she thought that this could be a way for her husband to escape the consequences of his sordid actions. Even after her breakdown her default is still based on seeking out her societally constructed White privilege. In which her desires are always the most important factor, even when someone was nearly killed.

It was an absolute blessing that he survived but nonetheless this tragedy should've never happened in the first place. He should've been questioned on his intentions without being gunned down at first sight due to his biological reality as a Black person. As if the endless stereotypes of cultural manipulation made it okay to brand him as a bad guy without getting to know him.

As everyone started to get ready to go home, another blast caused a symphony of ringing sounds to erupt from everyone's phone. At first no one dared to check since we were all terrified that it was yet another message from The Beast Of Liberty. Everyone simply looked around sharing highly anxious facial expressions, all of us highly unsure of what to do next.

Shaniece was the first who dared to look at her phone, she told us it wasn't him but rather the prodigal daughter herself. Hannah Maxwell went live for the first time in weeks and invited everyone in her list of contacts. How I was one of them was a mystery beyond my reasoning.

Apparently she was in the community center, according to Shaniece who recognized the lighting of the setting as she's taken several livestreams there herself. Hannah looked absolutely stunning as she wore a stunning blue dress that beautifully clashed with her fiery red hair. The darker toned lighting creating an eerie vibe that instantly made it seem like a highly disturbing stream. The wall behind her had a quote in a scary, bloody red color.

"Since mankind's dawn, a handful of oppressors have accepted the responsibility over our lives that we should have accepted for ourselves.

By doing so, they took our power. By doing nothing, we gave it away.

We've seen where their way leads, through camps and wars, towards the slaughterhouse."

NO JUSTICE
NO PEACE
BLM

CHAPTER 9:

To Feel True Love's Sting.

Narrator: Hannah Maxwell

"I had crossed the line. I was free; but there was no one to welcome me to the land of freedom. I was a stranger in a strange land."

Harriet Tubmann

9.1 THE HIGHEST LEVEL OF EXPOSURE

Hannah wasted no time whatsoever to share her message with the people following her stream. She started with letting everyone know that she was in a secret relationship with Deshawn, they were in love with each other and planned their entire future together. In the same naive way most young ones experience the powerful addiction more popularly referred to as romance.

She then went on to talk about his death, apparently she was there when he got shot. Hannah saw with her own eyes how Deshawn's soul left his vessel, it was such a horrific sight that broke her soul far beyond any chances of repair. But the worst was yet to come for it wasn't Deandre who killed him.

It was her father Dylan Maxwell who pulled the trigger on him, but it wasn't a targeted hit. Dylan was gunning for someone else and they were just in the wrong place at the wrong time which was how he got caught in the crossfire. A young man with so much potential and so much value in his community taken from his life by a stray bullet? I swear sometimes life seems just like an eternally cruel joke, with its punchline being that we humans keep existing in it even if we deserve extinction.

She exposed her father for what he was, a dangerous product of his racially abusive environment. Since the goggles of childhood ignorance that kept making him seem better than he actually was no longer fit her. For Hannah was clearly done with Dylan and his disturbingly evil character. She truly wanted him to pay for his actions. consequences be damned for his legacy.

After exposing the truth, Hannah then continued to dance around the room, seemingly engaging in a romantic ceremony with the spirit of her dead lover. I'm not sure what she's on right now, but it must be very powerful given the spacy dancing paired with facial expressions that clearly show a broken soul in search of a permanent escape from the darkness of this world. It was clear that the harsh truth of the man she loved being killed by the man who raised her was too much for to handle as she continued to aimlessly move around the room.

All the while, everyone in the hospital waiting room was glued to their screen, completely unable to believe what they had just heard directly from her mouth. Even Hannah's mother Katie couldn't process what she had just heard during that bizarre livestream. She looked at aunt Jasmine for a split second, before the pressure of looking right in her raging eyes was too much to handle. So she bowed her head in absolute shame and even refused to let head nurse Joy come closer to check on her wounds, it was like she wanted to remain bloody and in pain to make amends for her evil husband's actions.

Even though I probably shouldn't, I still couldn't help but feel bad for Katie, her life was crumbling down in front of our eyes and there was nothing that she could do about it. But then, I turned my head towards aunt Jasmine and I realized that the pain felt by Katie was a miraculous relief compared to the pain that she had to carry with her day in and day out. But little did I know that Katie's suffering was about to catch up because of yet another deadly curveball…

9.3 WHEN LIFE HANGS BY A THREAD

Even though Hannah was dancing we could only see her face and shoulders on the screen, which was a deliberate strategy that she used to shock us all with the destructive element of surprise. Because she was hiding something very disturbing behind her message of public exposure, one that would permanently affect both her life and the lives of everyone around her. When she stopped dancing she lifted up her arms and the very sight of that deadly image made everyone in the waiting room either gasp or scream. Especially her mother screamed so loud that it made my heart skip several beats in a row.

Apparently she had slit her wrists so deep, that the blood was dripping from her fingertips onto her cobalt dress. The glamorous shot was so mesmerizing that it almost distracted me from the seriousness of her suicidal actions. She held out her arms and kept staring at the camera with a lost, little smile which made it very clear that the Maxwell heir was beyond saving. She was over of this broken, messed up world and lost all hope for its restoration, Hannah simply wanted to join her lover towards a new journey beyond the limited borders of life.

One where they could finally be together again, one where her family wouldn't end up ruining both her life and the lives of Deshawn and his family. One where she could have what she wanted without having to go on with life forever missing the one person who made her feel seen, valued, heard and loved. Hannah had enough and she distracted us with her message long enough to make it nearly impossible to save her, but nurse Joy was still going to try her best to get an ambulance there.

ANOTHER SHOCKING REVELATION 9.4

As the paramedics were rushing their way to the community center, we were all treated to yet another disturbing surprise. Hannah had already dropped to the floor by then, but we could still hear her cries of mourning. When she stopped making noise everyone thought she was gone, then we heard loud footsteps as if someone deliberately wanted us to know Hannah wasn't alone.

Then the camera was picked up from its setting, and the holder aimed it at Hannah's body that was visibly losing life by the second. Everyone in the room cried and begged to stop the bleeding so she could survive. But our cries were simply ignored as Hannah continued to bleed out in front of everyone following her livestream.

Katie never stopped sending messages begging to help, but it was clear thar her messages were destined to be left on read. Whoever was filming had no intention to save this girl from dying, and just when Hannah's eyes started to close did the camera angle flip to shock us all.

It was The Beast Of Liberty yet again, this man never seems to get tired when death and destruction is on his highly disturbing mind. He didn't speak, all he did was stare directly into the phone camera to creep us all out. To be honest, it really worked as everyone felt so scary, especially the members of The Justice Collective. This was the first time they saw someone wear their mask and feel bad about the message it was representing.

And in one swift move, the mask was lifted to reveal the face of a young man who had seen too much evil.

9.5 ENTER THE BURDEN OF PROOF

He finally started to make some noise, but he was speaking in very chaotic tongues, talking about his plans having changed and that he couldn't wait to reveal his face to the world. I still had no idea who he was until I studied the faces of everyone around me, they all knew who he was, and they all seemed shocked by the revelation.

As I kept staring at his face, I started getting flashbacks about my visit to Creeper's Corner. To be more specific the flashbacks were about Tasha Fredricks, he had the same face as hers. A brownish skin tone matched with hazel eyes, full lips and a bone structure for days. The resemblance was so uncanny that he couldn't just be a distant relative, it simply had to be her son Deandre.

This boy really shot his own mother in the head in cold blood, with seemingly no remorse for his actions whatsoever. Not only that, he also lifted the brainwashing that kept Dylan Maxwell in check. Which led to him spiraling when he encountered Kieran under dubious circumstances. He's truly stopped caring about the people he loves, not even being bothered by using them as a sacrificial pawn or shooting practice.

When I was piecing the blood link together I had completely phased out of the livestream. Unaware of what crazy messages that Deshawn was spewing. When my attention finally switched back to my screen, he was crouching on the ground, putting his face next to Hannah's knowing it would give Dylan an even bigger fuel of rage. Surely he knew that Hannah had livestreamed everyone in her surroundings before bidding farewell?

This revelation has only taken a couple of minutes of our time, but it was such a heavy moment that it felt like more than just one day had passed. We were all shook to such an extent that nothing seemed real anymore, even Hannah's nightmare seemed to be fantasy in our eyes.

But it was very much a reality as the girl continued to bleed out with no help whatsoever from Deandre. He got back up, grabbed his mask again and put it on. Even when the secret's out, seeing him in his mask completes the outfit that simply hits different. He then delivered a message that clearly showed the greater agenda at play.

"If life is supposed to be a game where race, privilege and status have the power to take the board away.

Then how could you not expect vessels like me to get trapped in a system that pushes thuggery as a gateway?

But trust me when I tell you that my actions will turn me into the catalyst for this nation's ultimate civil disruption.

That will make every single faction in this game rise up to protest the current world order in a massive eruption.

Since now, the jig is up and no more revelations of law enforcement's cover-ups can be branded as hearsay."

He then cut off the camera, probably perfectly timing his getaway plan, as I have a feeling the worst is yet to come. What else could he still possibly have planned besides making sure that Dylan would be no more?

9.7 WHEN PIECES FALL INTO PLACE

Apparently, the livestream made sure that it wasn't just the ambulance rushing its way to the community center. So were a bunch of reporters and a stream of police vehicles, it became a late night news bulletin that shocked everyone. This time around, nurse Joy put on the tv in the waiting room and turned up the volume so everyone could hear the news report. By the time the ambulance arrived Hannah was no longer alive, there was nothing they could do besides pronounce her time of death.

Katie immediately dropped to the ground, crying her heart out as nurse Joy and everyone else around shared her pain. They may all hate her, but it was clear that her daughter Hannah was well-loved among both parents and children. This was a loss for every single one of them, even Shaniece seemed like her soul had been crushed by the livestream she had just witnessed.

But this time around, Kieran wasn't there to raise up everyone's spirit. He was still resting from the journey of survival located at the intersection between life and death. Shaniece kept feeling worse until she felt a panic attack coming up, to which the members of the collective responded by escorting her outside so she could get some fresh air in her system. None of the adults thought anything of it, they just continued to sit there and wallow in their own misery. It seemed like the best thing to do since all hope was truly lost at the moment.

A few minutes later, an ambulance driver ran into the waiting room, and then we realized it was a ploy since he told us that they distracted him and stole his vehicle.

The parents wasted no time and ran towards their cars, they thought that they knew their children better than the young ones themselves who still had a lot to learn about life. While that may be true, kids are also much smarter than we adults give them credit for. They set off on a collective ride towards the community center, thinking that's where the ambulance went. But little did they know that the kids were headed somewhere else.

Kiara confirmed my suspicion rather quickly, as we were the only ones left behind, aunt Jasmine joined the parent gang on their journey. While nurse Joy had taken Katie to a separate room to check on her vitals. Kiara told me to go online and check Shaniece's socials, she had the highest following out of everyone in the collective so it made sense that she would post something.

And she did, she let her followers know that The Justice Collective was headed towards Deacon Valley's police department and she invited all of her followers to join them. I guess the reveal of the police cover-up made Shaniece so mad that it made her seek out some sort of confrontation. But both Kiara and I feared for her safety, and wanted to follow up so we could keep a guardian eye on all of them. However, Kiara couldn't bring herself to get up, she felt obligated to stay here until her brother Kieran would finally wake up.

I still had the keys to the van and she told me to go on this journey alone, the car rides we shared earlier were enough for her to trust me. It was now my task to make sure that they would all be safe from harm.

9.9 A STAMPEDE AT THE PRECINCT

I wanted to drive just as fast as when I rushed Kiara to the hospital, but this time around I was alone and scared beyond reason that a cop would decide to pull me over. So by the time that I had arrived, Shaniece and the rest of the members were already there, but they weren't alone. There were a vast number of people protesting at the precinct, in all shapes, colors and sizes with a clear message to the members of the precinct.

Eventually, I was able to locate Shaniece and the others who were rushing their way forward, hoping to get front seats to witness the turmoil. Shaniece had a determined look in her eyes, that she would not shy away from confrontation. She was going to protest as if her life depended on it, this was her way of coping with everything.

At the front of the protest, Darius was there alongside a woman in police uniform. She had brownish skin, with long curly hair that she tied up to resemble a samurai bun. She seemed very familiar with Darius so I'm guessing they have some sort of history together. Shaniece let me know that her name was Daniela Johnson, she was an officer of the law, and an active warrior in the seemingly endless fight for police reform. She was fighting for more than a decade hoping it would knock off police chief Tanner from his privileged and abusive throne.

In the past it always failed, but his time around, the scales had tipped in Daniela's favor, as now she had both the predominantly White women on her side as well as the men of color. Giving her an edge that could finally make her visions of a better law enforcement come true.

The cheers kept getting louder while Darius & Daniela continued to rile them up. At the entrance, a Caucasian officer with a large posture and a constant angry facial expression stood watch. He seemed very jumpy, as if he was expecting chaos to happen so he tried to keep his calm to hopefully avoid any panic induced mistakes.

He continued to look at all of us with such a visible sense of fear, but was he afraid that we would attack him then and there? Or was he fearful of the reality that law enforcement's golden days of oppression and turning blind eyes were coming to an end? Either way, the fact that he displayed so much fear clearly meant that we were making a serious impact on the powers that be and their unjustified rule of oppression.

How terrible it must feel to be in police chief Tanner's shoes right now as the ground beneath him is starting to shake. Making his ridiculously high walls of privilege collapse at a swift pace, exposing nothing but the puny little man behind the shield who held on to his throne for way too long. He was done for, as his reputation took such a hard beating that it forever tainted his image with signs that labeled his character as nothing more than weak.

When we saw Tanner curiously peeking out his nosy head through his office window, it became clear that he wasn't planning on having any meaningful conversations tonight. So we all gathered, and started to loop the mantra of The Justice Collective, the same mantra that Kieran used earlier today. The mantra spread like wildfire to every activist until it was halted by a loud bang!

NO JUSTICE
NO PEACE
BLM

CHAPTER 10:

To Balance A Broken Scale.

Narrator: Madeline Tanner

"A child cannot be taught by
anyone who despises him,
and a child cannot afford
to be fooled."

James Baldwin

10.1 MADNESS AT THE PRECINCT

The bang was so loud and shocking that everyone knew a gun had been fired. It incited a massive wave of panic as the protesters assumed that a sniper was taking them out from a bird's eye point of view. But then, we heard screams coming from inside the precinct, calming us down while also raising all of our curiosity levels.

The officer protecting the gate instantly sounded the alarm out of sheer sense of panic, causing a violent stream of bright lights to erupt with an overload of high pitch noises. This triggered me to have flashbacks to the motel parking lot, when Kiara buried her face on my shoulder to avoid the impact of these migraine inducing lights. But there was no escaping it as the alarm automatically resulted in a lockdown at the precinct.

Everyone had to stay inside to investigate whether or not an intruder was present and to also prevent his chances of escape. At least that's the feedback that the reporters were given when they asked the officer standing at the gate. At first he did a good job to keep us calm, but then he received some news through his walkie talkie that visibly crushed his soul. He collapsed to the ground and at that point one of the reporters received news from a 'credible' source inside that the victim was police chief Tanner. He had apparently killed himself using a gun that he's owned since his very start as a patrol officer. A beretta, the same weapon that's been used all weekend to bring us nothing but pain and a seemingly eternal sense of suffering. At first, everyone was skeptical of the news, but the officer on the ground was so distraught that he confirmed it to be the truth...

Right after the distraught officer confirmed the news of the suicide, a vehicle was headed towards the parking at an extremely fast pace. It was Principal Tanner, who instantly jumped out of her car, clearly already aware that something was wrong. Even though we had just found out the news ourselves, she already seemed aware of the fact that something was wrong. Maybe her husband had sent her a final message before eating his own beretta?

It was disturbingly awkward to see her so distraught and frightened, the nightgown and flip flops that she was wearing were a stark contrast from the professional Barbara Stinson look I saw her in earlier today. I could tell that I wasn't the only one who couldn't fit the picture with the image they had of Madeline Tanner as a person.

She didn't even have to storm through the masses, as everyone immediately stepped out of her way when she came closer. Even Shaniece and the rest of the students didn't want the smoke that she was capable of releasing at this point in time. When she arrived at the gate, the press immediately started to trail her so they could film this confrontation for everyone in the valley to see.

"WHERE IS HE!
LET ME SEE HIM!
NOW!!!"

She shouted at the officer while completely unaware of the camera's surrounding her. When the officer told her the news she instantly fell on his shoulder in tears while the camera's continued to feed off of her suffering.

10.3 THE REALITY OF PALATABILITY

For years, officer Daniela Johnson was gunning for a seat at the head of the table, so she could finally bring reform to a system designed to be broken for all eternity. All the while she had to face abuse from all sides because of her status as a double minority due to her race and gender. Now there was finally enough outrage that she could actually convince hearts and minds to trust in her potential. Only to have that trust stripped away from her when police chief Tanner decided to end his own life.

Within a short time frame, she went from a nobody, to a possible savior and now she was the ultimate big bad of Deacon Valley's traditional seat of power. All because the victimized tears of Madeline Tanner demonized her public image to a point of no return. Even the protesters couldn't help but see her as the source of this powerful White woman's pain and the reason for the powerful White man's suicide. Both her skin complexion and her womanhood were instantly seen as 'threatening' to the masses of people surrounding the precinct.

If she was White, she could've been spared from this status as an undesirable effigy and if she were a man she could take that sense of danger and use it to her advantage as a power play. But given the fact that she was neither there was nothing she could say or do to shake off the negative vibe that everyone received from her.

It seems like no matter how you twist or turn it, there is never a way out for us women of color specifically. As if we were the only crabs in the barrel that weren't allowed to escape because societies love to serve us on a plate.

As Madeline continued to cry on the officer's shoulder, the entrance gate suddenly swung open. Much to my surprise, it was Dylan who walked out of the building. Apparently, he wasn't at the community center as we all expected. So there was a chance that he didn't know about his daughter's suicide yet. Since this particular protest at the precinct started before Hannah's livestream.

Dylan walked past a sobbing Principal Tanner, stepped up to both the protesters and the reporters so he could deliver the news of police chief Tanner's suicide. He was calm, empathetic and seemed a bit too composed for my liking. Surely, Dylan didn't think that he could find a way to escape punishment and become the chief himself?

Given all the messed up exposures that I've witnessed today, I probably wouldn't be shocked if this ended up being the case. He was so composed that it made the protesters lose their drive while it simultaneously amped up the reporters to ask simple questions that would lean towards law enforcement's favor. But then came the question that rocked his world, the one about Hannah.

"What do you mean? What happened to my daughter?"

The officer that was busy consoling Principal Tanner then approached Dylan with his phone in hand. He showed him the stream and based on the sudden shift of Dylan's mood, it was clear that he was seeing Hannah's death and the unmasking of Deandre Fredricks as The Beast Of Liberty. All Dylan could do was stare at everyone as they kept shoving their camera's in his face.

10.5 YET ANOTHER COP TRAGEDY

Dylan was still frozen still, unable to respond to the barrage of questions being thrown at him, while the flashing camera lights visibly started to annoy him. It was clear that he was done with the situation so when questions surrounding the night of the Juneteenth party started coming in he immediately lost it. Never have I seen someone make use of so much deflection that it actually made them confused about what's real and what's fake.

The officer next to him decided to intervene, he started interrupting the questions and got very defensive when the 'wrong' questions were being asked. Questions that threatened to disrupt the image that Deacon Valley P.D. had among the citizens it was bound to protect & serve. It was clear that he felt threatened that the death of police chief Tanner also meant the death of his undeserved privileges at the precinct. He would no longer have that going on for him considering the fact that everyone was now starting to see the seemingly endless problematic realities of law enforcement. And that fear made him say things with a vague, underlying meaning behind it.

When Daniela Jonson decided to open her mouth it was game over for him. He immediately tried to silence her and when she refused he approached her at a rapid pace. Everyone thought they would simply have an up-close screaming match, but his plans were more homicidal than argumentative. As soon as he got close enough, he reached for his gun, but Daniela was also a trained officer with cat-like reflexes so she reached for her gun just as fast. As soon as their aim was on lock they simultaneously fired a round & it was a headshot for both parties.

DYLAN'S WORLD CRASHING DOWN 10.6

Within the span of half an hour, three police officers died with no outside parties involved. Two officers killed each other while the chief killed himself as he already knew his department had become a sinking ship that was beyond the possibility of saving. So far this day kept getting worse by the second, a part of me was happy to know that it was almost over. While another part of me was deeply concerned that there was still way more deadly damage to be done before the arrival of midnight.

You should've seen the look on Dylan's face when he saw me in the crowd alongside Shaniece. I truly thought that he was also about to snap just like the others. But to my surprise he stayed real calm and looked the opposite way, letting me know that I was spared, for now at least...

Even though I was relieved to be safe at that time, there was still a voice in my head yelling at me to get the hell out of dodge. A voice that fueled my panic even more than my mother's final message to me when she took over Kieran's vessel. A voice begging me to leave this valley before I got sucked into this disturbing madness with no chance of escape whatsoever. But the only issue was that the voice was warning me of a possibility that was already a reality since I had no intention of leaving.

Even though I've been here for less than 48 hours, I've grown connected to this place to such an extent that I can't just let it go. Even if it meant risking death, I will stay here and make sure that justice is served. The great exposure may have set the first phase in motion, but there are still quite a few difficult steps left to take.

10.7 EXPOSURE TO SOCIETY

With both officers dead on the ground, the people needed someone new to demonize, someone that they could hold responsible for everything going wrong. Someone who was deemed evil enough in plain sight so any form of blame and responsibility could easily be projected onto them. And since Dylan Maxwell was clearly at the center of all this damn controversy, it's only fair that he be the bad guy now.

For once in his overly privileged life, Dylan knew what it felt like to have all eyes on him in the most negative way imaginable. For once he was the one that was seen as a threat by everyone even if not a single person made an effort to get to know him. He was now the bad guy and no matter what he said or did, it would be twisted to make him look even worse than he already did.

Never again would the people fall for his ridiculously fake version of masculine 'charm'. Nor would they fall for his attempts to strong-arm someone while making it appear noble in the eyes of the public. He was finally judged by the content of his obviously disturbing character, rather than the privileged reality of his race. If this is what true justice feels like, then sign me up for life.

Since this is what I want for Dylan Maxwell, I want him to have no place whatsoever where he can feel loved, accepted and rewarded for his nature. He had to feel shamed, hated and targeted no matter where he was, never in his life should he feel a moment of peace. Since he has caused both his enemies and his loved ones to feel nothing but a destructive sense of pain.

It's clear that Kieran has left a permanent mark on the precinct after the stunt he pulled earlier today. Since it clearly went viral for a reason, it really stuck with people. Since every protester was really stuck on the meaning behind his message, it was so powerful that they began to repeat it. Except this time around, it wasn't The Justice Collective alone doing it, so they slightly tweaked it to fit the greater narrative of allyship in times of need.

"Remember, remember the 26th of February where a Black one was killed with the offensive firing of a shot!

For 10 years later still no one has found a way to change the system so that **their** lives are no longer left to rot!"

The message was spoken in such unison that it created a noise that no one could ignore. It brought together residents from different worlds, to fight with a united sense humanity for the one & only element that binds us as a society, **Justice**. All eyes were aimed on Dylan who had to endure the cries while standing there looking like an oppressive fool. It became too much for him and something inside snapped, he pulled out his gun, aimed it at the sky and fired several rounds! Everyone stopped chanting and immediately started screaming instead. It created such a frenzy where everyone was pushing each other out of the way to get the hell out of dodge.

It was chaos and panic all around, the members of the collective ran towards the ambulance, while Shaniece looked for safety in her father's arms. Leaving me exposed in chaos, with a possible killer coming for me.

10.9 EXIT THROUGH THE RIFT SHOP

I froze in my tracks, with no idea what to do next, all the while Dylan continued to stand with his gun still pointing at the sky. If there was ever a way of telling someone that you're on a massive power trip without actually telling someone then this would be it. My mind was sending so many signals towards my body to move, but it felt like I was stuck on mute for an undetermined period time.

When Dylan finally put his gun back in his holster, a stream of officers came running through the entrance to establish order from the absolute chaos. Something about seeing all of those officers run out scared me enough to finally regain control of my body. I started running away and this must've caught his attention since he began to chase me like a true predator.

I was running for my life while praying to any higher power that could hear me to keep me from falling by Dylan's disgustingly unjust hands. I'm not sure who responded, but whoever it was had a very particular sense of humor. Since it was Principal Tanner who decided to serve as my knight in anything but shining armor.

She pulled up in her car & told me to get in, even though I dreaded the idea of sharing a ride with her it was still better than the alternative of becoming yet another element of a deeply sinister cop killing statistic. I got inside and she wasted no time driving off while Dylan stood there in complete shock. Never in a million years would Dylan have guessed that Madeline Tanner would rescue me. To be totally honest, neither did I so clearly there was something wrong with this highly suspicious picture.

I couldn't explain what I was feeling during that car ride, it was like the emotions were impossible to describe with the limited definitions of words. That's a constant for a lot of the emotions that I've experienced on this near timeless weekend of chaos with extra madness on top.

On the one hand I felt somewhat relieved to be saved from that policing spawn of Satan, even though Dylan was coocoo for all sorts of cocoa puffs right now. I knew he would never follow us, since he wouldn't dare to risk Madeline's Tanner's life. But on the other hand, I felt so uncomfortable to be inside her car, a woman whom I could tell was not a fan of people like me. Though she would never admit it, it was clear that Madeline Tanner did not believe in the equal value of humanity since it clashed with the sense of supremacy belonging to her Caucasian identity. It was so clear that I hesitated for several minutes before I dared to ask where we were going.

"We're going to see a man that I need to speak to, a man who knew all of this would happen.

He told me long ago that one day everyone in this valley would feel pain beyond both measure and healing.

I want to know how he knew about our fall as a society."

I had no idea who she was talking about, I kept staring outside of the window to avoid any type of contact with her. All the while I wondered who it could possibly be, who could this man be that warned Madeline of the moment that Deacon Valley suffered beyond imagination?

NO JUSTICE
NO PEACE
BLM

CHAPTER 11:

To Defy
All Tradition.

Narrator: Gabriel Ramirez

"It is not our differences that divide us. It is our inability to recognize, accept & celebrate those differences."

Audre Lorde

11.1 FULFILLING GINA'S FINAL WISH

The entire ride I wondered who the mystery man could be, as I kept staring out of the window we approached a small diner. The lighting inside was terrible, but the outside had a beautifully dark vibe to it due to the bright neon light sign standing on a pedestal alongside a statue.

It was shaped like a voluptuous woman with an afro haired pattern, with a sign in her hands of the diner's name, "The Rapid Valley". My mind had already been completely destroyed by today's events, so it took me a second to put two and two together. It was the name of the diner that I ordered my food from yesterday, I guess now is the time to fulfill Gina's last wish.

As we were about to talk to her son Gabriel, the little boy I dreamt of last night and the delivery guy who was the first one to help me see the unreal foundations of Deacon Valley's eternally fake empire. It's funny how fate always seemed to be one step ahead of us, no matter how much we anticipated for things. Life was always ready to throw in the plot twist that could destroy any and every aspect of our lives.

Madeline parked the car, but she was too hesitant to take the keys out of the ignition. She just stared at her steering wheel while clutching it for dear life, until she spoke.

"This was a bad idea, I shouldn't have come here."

Just as I was about to ask her why she continued.

"Get out, NOW!"

I listened to her demand and stepped out of the car, leaving her to drive away with such an intense speed. At least she got me out of harm's way so Madeline deserved some credit for that, even though she bailed on a mission that she started without my knowledge nor consent. But talking to Gabriel was on my list anyway so in the end it went according to plan after all.

As soon as I got close to the door, it swung right open giving me a clear view of the interior. It had a warm, homely feel to it, as if you not only entered an establishment but also someone's heart, mind and soul. Gabriel walked outside and looked me dead in the eyes while giving me a very warm, disarming smile.

"We've been expecting you.
Come on in, I have yesterday's order ready for you."

We? Who the hell is we? A part of me had no intention of finding that out, but in all honesty where the hell was I going to go at this hour? And I was feeling mad hungry so I could use some delicious food right now. I walked in and all of my anxious feelings turned into a flash of happiness lighting up my soul. It was Kiara sitting at the table and before I could ask she explained her presence.

"Nurse Joy dropped me off, I'm here on Kieran's orders.

When he woke up, he told me that he spoke to Deshawn and that I could find all of the answers I need here.

He also told me that I could expect a visit from you."

11.3 A CAUTIONARY TALE OF DARKNESS

I sat down next to Kiara while Gabriel ran to the kitchen so he could serve us a meal. After the day that we have both had, this moment almost feels like a final supper to fill our stomachs before the greatest tragedy will commence. Gabriel walked out of the kitchen and started to place the food on our table, it all smelled so good that I almost forgot about the deadly drama.

Gabriel then sat down and took off the rosary chain he wore around his neck and cupped it in his hands before saying grace in Spanish. Kiara and I bowed down our heads to show respect, and waited until he had finished before starting to eat. We both complimented him on the food and then Kiara suddenly grabbed her phone. She asked if she could record their conversation to which he nodded yes, she gave a short intro and then immediately asked Gabriel how he knew Deandre.

"Deandre and I are kindred spirits, mainly due to our similar childhoods on the wrong side of the track.

I always had a strong desire to see him succeed, and avoid falling in with the wrong crowds.

But given today's great exposure, it's very clear that I failed him in more ways than just one.

I guess now all that's left to do is give you the answers you need to make some good come out of all this bad.

Because if you know Deandre the way I do, then you'd realize that he always saves the best for last."

THE NIGHT OF JUNETEENTH 11.4

Deandre was a troubled, young boy who struggled with losing his father at the hands of those who were obligated to protect and serve. On the one hand, he grew up with an absolute sense of hatred for authority as he dreamed of punishing the system one day. But on the other hand, he also couldn't bear himself to enact pain on another living creature. Since he felt way too much of a connection to the sensitive side of being human.

He grew up developing both parts of himself as a split personality. Until one day the bad managed to take over the good as he had a plan to take down officers Dylan Maxwell and Devin Rogers. He had it set for the Juneteenth party where the Black community was known to invite guests from across the racial spectrum to celebrate and discuss this historic day. Seeing as how everyone would be way too occupied partying, it gave him ample opportunity to go dark side and do damage.

But sadly, he experienced a final lapse of his softer side and flinched when it mattered the most. Which eventually lead to the death of Deshawn Davis and the officers using him as the ultimate scapegoat for their evil actions.

This led Deandre to go absolutely mad with rage as he burst through Gabriel's door after the tragedy had unfolded. He cried his heart out to Gabriel as a way of dealing with the overload of emotions that came with the territory of survivor's guilt. He stayed with Gabriel for a few days and he noticed a change in his character. It was like Deandre no longer existed, leaving behind a hollow shell that required a mask to tell its story.

11.5 THE LIFE OF DEANDRE FREDRICKS

Deandre's grandmother always raised him with the idea that his parents were mistakenly judged for drug dealers. But as a teenager he was able to uncover the truth and learn for himself that his father was indeed dealing at Creeper's Corner. In fact, the anonymous tip was based on a bogus call placed by Dylan and Devin's associate.

They had planned the entire drug bust as a mere plot to end the competition once and for all. When Deandre figured all of this out he wanted revenge rage and planned a hit on all of them. He was able to convince their associate Old Man Ray to turn on them, by simply bribing him with a seat at the financially driven table.

But Deandre flinched when push came to shove and the situated turned against them. Deandre was able to escape but Dylan was hell-bent on making sure he was dealt with swiftly. Deandre was wearing the same hoodie and jeans as the ones belonging to his vigilante attire.

Sadly, Deshawn was wearing the same thing when he was on a nightly stroll his girl Hannah after they both abruptly ditched the party. Hannah wanted to take him to a small little field close to her grandparent's cabin. It was so dear to her heart because her family always took her there to play. It was also the place where Dylan and Devin would handle their dirty side business, sadly making Deshawn a potential target by default. What Hannah saw as a beautiful place that awakened her childhood nostalgia, Dylan saw as the perfect space to break the law and get away with it. In this case, the apple really did seem to fall far from the extremely disturbing tree.

THE LIFE OF RAYMOND BROWN 11.6

Old Man Ray was a veteran criminal who was born and raised in a home well-known for selling both drugs and sexual favors. Ever since he was a young kid he always had a gritty perspective of humanity. Since he was able to see both the pious public status and sinful personal image behind everyone in his area.

From a very young age, his visions for the future were bleak, he had no true hobby nor career aspirations. All Raymond truly cared about was chasing the paper by any means necessary. Leading him to a life of crime before he could even learn how to drive. But in all of his years hustling the corners of every street he was never sent to jail. Because he used to work as both an informant and a servant for the cops who preferred to abide by the dirtier side of the system.

Over time he managed to build a solid partnership with officers Dylan Maxwell and Devin Rogers. The poster boys for dirty cops who were always protected from harm due to the privilege they were given in life.

But he was paid peanuts compared to what the officers were stacking up in cash. So it shouldn't come as a total surprise that he was more than eager to help Deandre overthrow the demonic duo. But the plan backfired and when they couldn't get Deandre, they killed Raymond and blamed the entire operation on Deandre. Making Raymond's legacy vanish from Deacon Valley since no one in the valley wanted to be near him. They also hoped it would make Deandre skip town forever since no one would believe the truth, but they were wrong about that.

11.7 WHEN ENOUGH IS ENOUGH

When Gabriel started crying Kiara couldn't help but shut down the video, she believed that our pain had been exploited enough and anyone who didn't feel empathy for our struggle was simply incapable of doing so.

She saved the video recording and immediately published it to her feed, without a single edit being made. In her eyes, no amount of editing could compare to the ultimate power that was present in the gritty, raw truth. A message so unfiltered that no amount of disturbance could possibly lead to confusion.

By now it was already past midnight, so its true impact would probably come tomorrow. Giving Kiara the necessary time to prepare for the backlash of her decision to publish it for all of her followers to see. Shaniece was the first one to see the video, she didn't publicly respond, but simply liked while also sending Kiara a DM that made me hate the fact that this night wasn't over.

"Send me your location.
We need to meet ASAP!"

When Kiara saw that message she immediately sent Shaniece our location while also asking her what was going on. Apparently, the people weren't going to let Dylan's display of 51-50 slide without a reaction. The camera footage of that frenzy made the headline news and it went viral far beyond the borders of Deacon Valley. Activists all across the country were mad by what they had seen. This vocal support was exactly what the people needed to step up and take on the final stand.

Within minutes after posting the recorded interview, Kiara's feed blew up so intensely, the amount of messages pouring in were impossible to count. The people have clearly had enough of all the cover-ups that prevented actual justice from being served.

This transparent interview where Gabriel Ramirez dared to pour out his heart and soul was truly the last straw for so many. Everyone was claiming that this was the ultimate turning point in our history. Given the way this day played out, it truly seems like the ancestors have had enough of seeing their children continue to suffer from the consequences of their historic shackles.

By that logic every single death in this short period of time can be seen as nothing more than a sacrifice to break the pillars of society's hypocritical illusion spell. A spell so powerful that even the brightest minds can find themselves getting lost in the mesmerizing sauce. A spell with the ability to constantly gaslight your own personal experiences in favor of upholding the endless silence that exists to support a fictional greater good.

In all honesty, it wasn't a mere illusion spell, but rather a timeless curse deeply rooted in every single aspect of this world and its oppressive societal construction. A curse so poisonously evil that it enforced tyranny while also continuing to breed a rebellious sense of destruction. Surely, enough blood had been spilled already to lift this vile curse from our lives? Or was my mother being dead serious about an actual river of blood being spilled? Lord have mercy on us if the latter ends up being true.

11.9 THE CATAPULT OF RESISTANCE

Shaniece pulled up in the T.J.C. van just in time for Gabriel to close-up shop. We wasted no time and got in so we could get to the high school. Shaniece was saying that we had an errand to run before we were ready for tomorrow morning. She was acting very weird so we decided to ask her what the errand was and she replied.

"Last night we were going to protest at our graduation ceremony before Madeline canceled our plans.

It happened so fast that we couldn't even roll out our catapult of resistance.

So normally it should still be hidden in the school basement unless someone got to it already.

We're going to try and retrieve the catapult for tomorrow morning's all-defining protest."

Then she explained what the catapult of resistance was, it was a literal catapult that the students of Deacon Valley High had built as their 'secret' graduation project. It was a catapult built to launch a giant ball full of excerpts from the Black History month lessons. Articles, essays, quotes and philosophical teachings that would fall down on their targets like a wave of hard-hitting confetti.

Last night's original plan was to launch the catapult at the faculty members as a symbol of resistance to their oppressive rule. But now the idea was to launch it at the police officers that would try their very best to disband our protest, let's hope this doesn't end up going bad...

Just as we were about to leave, Gabriel decided that he couldn't let us go alone. After all, there were still two killers on the loose, one of them was an officer of the law while the other was a villain pushed to the side of evil due to the poisonous life that he lived. He wanted to make sure that he could keep us safe from harm, probably projecting his mother's death towards us. In his mind, he probably tried to overcompensate as a man for what he was unable to achieve as a boy.

There has to be more to that story, maybe this was a good idea for us to get the information that Kiara couldn't get him to say while she was recording. We all gave each other a quick look and agreed to let him join us, secretly I was even thrilled to know that someone else was going along for the ride. And though I still believe with all my heart in the devastating capacity of 'Stranger Danger', I was willing to overlook it with Gabriel. There was something about him that gave me the impression that I was safe around his presence.

He got in and sat next to me, while Shaniece and Kiara were sitting upfront, he seemed very calm even though we were headed on a mission that could bring major troubles with it. I asked him how he could stay calm and what he would actually do if one of them showed up at the school, to which he simply lifted up his shirt.

It seemed to be forever on brand that every man on a mission in Deacon Valley should carry a beretta. The same was the case for Gabriel, as he clearly showed us that he was packing a potentially homicidal heat.

NO JUSTICE
NO PEACE
BLM

CHAPTER 12:

To Settle An Unjust Score.

Narrator: Deandre Fredricks

"You can't separate peace
from freedom because no
one can be at peace unless
he has his freedom."

Malcolm X

12.1 GABRIEL'S TRUE MOTIVATION

On our way to the school, Gabriel caught the sudden case of the gum flap blues. He started talking about his life and finally revealed the tea of his life story. When he was a little kid he used to live with his grandmother since his mother Gina was sadly one of the many victims in this country's opioid crisis. Though she loved her son very much, she just wasn't able to take care of him.

Joseph Maxwell's sister Jane also had an addiction similar to Gina's, they had the same dealer who was known for steering his product towards gullible young women. He knew that Jane had a brother who was a cop but that still didn't stop him from selling to her as he liked to live on the edge. One day, Jane was craving the fix a little too much and she ended up overdosing.

It sent Joseph down a tailspin in which he had to destroy the man responsible for his sister's death. No strategies were off limits, so he started using Gina Ramirez to do his bidding. He baited her with false motivations of helping her get clean for little Gabriel, but in reality he was simply using her as an informant. And when he collected enough intel, he went in for the kill without making sure that Gina was safe first, which eventually led to her slow, painful death by the hands of his henchmen.

Now that I've received the full scope of the story I truly understand why The Maxwells were killed. Deandre did it as a way of honoring Gabriel whom he felt close to. It wasn't just about making Dylan hurt, the motivations were a lot more personal. And to be honest, Joseph and Lisa Maxwell truly did have it coming in the end.

When we got close to the school, we saw a car driving behind us , it looked like it started to pick up speed, as if we were the intended targets of a road rage assault. The closer the car got, the more we realized it was a police vehicle, this made all of our hearts instantly sink to our stomachs. The siren went off and we were given the signal to stop, Shaniece didn't hesitate as she knew the alternative would be much, much worse.

We pulled over to the side of the road and so did the police vehicle, for a second we all just sat there waiting for something to happen. It was almost like the officer was deliberately trying to mess with our anxiety levels, as if he wanted to see us squirm. When the officer stepped out of the car it turned out to be The Beast Of Liberty.

"DRIVE, NOW!" Gabriel shouted at Shaniece, who wasted no time by putting pedal to the metal so we could be out of that situation. But sadly, Deandre was already prepared with his Beretta in hand. He fired several shots, the first two shots burst open the back window while the third hit Gabriel in the back of the head. This instantly killed him, making all of us go crazy as Shaniece continued to step on the gas so the three of us could get out of harm's way.

Then, he fired two more rounds, aimed at the tires, the first one missed but the second one clipped the back left tire making Shaniece lose control of the vehicle. She tried her best to get it back but it wasn't meant to be since she steered from the road and knocked the van straight into a tree, causing all of us to black out.

12.3 THE UNNECESSARY TIME-JUMP

When we woke up, it was already morning, the van was already exposed for several hours to the solar power of Dawn's light. So by this point, Gabriel's corpse had already started decaying beyond the point of smelling musty. As soon as we were fully awake, it only took one whiff of that terrible smell to make us jump out of that van. Which only made a flock of cameras and reporters approach us with questions we weren't ready to answer.

We were still trying to process what happened to us while the reporters had a field day pressing us while we were in a vulnerable, defenseless state of mind.

It was weird to see no cops present at the scene, especially since one of their own was probably missing and most certainly dead by now. How else would Deandre have been able to drive that cop car last night? And why on earth didn't he just finish us off? Why did he just leave us there for our survival to be left in fate's hands?

So many questions but no time to discuss them as Kiara and Shaniece were stuck with seemingly no way out. Luckily, I was overlooked and spared from their nosiness. Giving me ample opportunity to slip away and steal a play from The Justice Collective's book of schemes. I scouted the cars and noticed one where the keys were still in the ignition. So I hopped in with nothing but blind confidence, approached the swarm of reporters while Shaniece and Kiara were immediately on board and jumped right in the car. We drove off as the reporters ran back to their vehicles so they could chase us. The same way a paparazzi follows around the brightest star.

Hungry, confused and traumatized would be the best way to describe the three of us right now. I was driving faster than I ever had in my life, but that was simply to get the reporters off our trail. In reality, I had no idea where we were going, it took a little bit for our phones to get a decent signal. When it finally did happen, both Kiara & Shaniece's phones blew up for different reasons.

Shaniece was getting messages that thanked her for making sure that the catapult of resistance was at the protest. Even though we had no idea where the protest was at. None of us knew a damn thing about anything!

While Kiara was being stalked by Nurse Joy who called her several times throughout the night. After listening to a few messages, her face instantly froze in a manic state of both panic and fear. Apparently, Kieran's condition had suddenly shifted and his chances of recovery were in limbo yet again. She snapped out of it rather quickly and immediately called her back, but no one answered.

The shocking news broke us all as tears started streaming from our eyes, Shaniece even stopped reading the messages of the protest. She just stared out in front of her, wondering which road to take. On the one hand, we wanted to join the protesters so we could see Deshawn's final wish of the great catapult launching come true. But on the other hand, we had to get to the hospital to see if Kieran was okay or even alive for that matter. For even Deshawn would've abandoned the protest if he were still alive and in the same situation. Especially if it meant being there for his dying brother from another mother.

12.5 A GATHERING UNLIKE ANY OTHER

With my fast driving, it didn't take us long to arrive at the hospital, there we witnessed something that completely destroyed Kiara and caused her to scream so loudly that it burst my eardrums. All the members of The Justice Collective stood outside with candles in their hands as if they were at a vigil, which could only be done for Kieran. So the worst possible outcome had become a horrifying reality, a bitter truth that neither Kiara nor Shaniece were ready to swallow. Even I had difficulty accepting it and I barely knew this young man, so that should say enough about the extremely high level of sadness.

We got out of the van and immediately ran towards them, Kiara demanded to see her brother, no matter how hard it would be to stare at his decaying corpse. But it was then that the disturbingly dark mood was suddenly lifted, as the members confirmed that he was still alive and doing well. He recovered yet again and was now in the process of resting up, everyone was standing outside to thank the staff for providing good care to Kieran.

When nurse Joy couldn't reach Kiara she started contacting everyone else hoping they could help, but none of them knew where we were. So they all decided to abandon the plan and came here to offer support, even though Kieran was busy fighting for his life, they believed that his spirit would appreciate the family love.

It was then that Shaniece realized that all the messages she had received came from her former classmates, but none of them were from the collective. They were simply praising her for inspiring them to raise their voice.

After Kiara was finally able to calm down and get herself together, we walked inside of the hospital to see nurse Joy running around like a lunatic. She was urging her fellow nurses to prepare as much as they could, since they were expecting all of their beds to be occupied by the end of today. When Joy saw us she immediately ran towards Kiara and hugged her so tight that it made me feel like I was being suffocated with so much love.

Though it was a beautiful moment, I still had to interrupt and ask her why she thought the beds would be occupied. She simply grabbed the remote and turned on the tv in the lobby, there we saw the reporters that we were able to shake a little while ago. They were now live at the scene of the protest, except it had turned into a full blown riot after one of the officers maced an older woman who collapsed to the ground because of it.

They were at the Trinity square, breaking down any and everything that stood in their way. Even the officers at the first line of defense were no match for the protesters who here looking for an ultimate confrontation. After seeing this, I understood why Joy was preparing for every possible outcome, since this had a very big chance of going sour. Deacon Valley was in the final stages of an ultimate societal collapse, one where no one would manage to evade the consequences tied to such a tragic event. The destruction of the current power structure was a no brainer at this point. The only real questions that remained unanswered were which new power structure would replace the current one? And would it actually achieve better results for every member of society?

12.7 A CLASH OF ALL IDENTITIES

Just when I thought I had seen it all, Deacon Valley managed to surprise me yet again. I had no idea this was a place of so many different people. If there ever existed something like a true spectrum of diversity, then this is what it would look like in my opinion.

So many different groups of differing opinions, known to often clash with each other for the dumbest reasons you could possibly imagine. Forever being pitted together by their oppressors so that their dominance over all of us may never fade. But this time around, they all joined forces to clash against the establishment that continued to hold them down. Hoping that it may finally break the chains of history's seemingly endless repetition.

Even though all of the events that led up to this moment were filled with nothing but tragedy and pain. It didn't take away the beauty of that moment where all of our stories as humans come together. A moment where we all realized that overcoming the greater war was far more important than the near perverted obsession with the petty victory of the smaller battle.

It seemed almost too good to be true, especially for Kiara, Shaniece and the others who stared at the screen in complete disbelief. They never believed that unity was possible, so they never prepared for this outcome. On the one hand, it gave them hope for a better future. But on the other hand, they were also skeptical of this sudden merging of traditionally warring factions. Something in the back of their minds, told them that this could also be a mere performative display of braindead solidarity.

We had no idea how, but the catapult that we were going to retrieve last night was right there alongside the protesters. And given the endless stream of messages that Shaniece received, it was more than clear that everyone thought we did it. Which was impossible given the fact that neither of us would have been able to get to the school, retrieve the catapult and then come back to the scene of the crime and go back to sleep in the exact same spot as when we blacked out. There was just no way that was the case, which means it was either an unknown guardian angel or that infamous vigilante devil.

They were preparing to launch the ball at the police, this made Shaniece jump out from the back of the car so she could see it better. She immediately started streaming the moment alongside Kiara who did the same for maximum exposure. Everyone had to be given the chance to witness history being made after all, even if there was still a long road ahead of us. The protesters at the scene proudly started chanting loud cheers of rebellion while urging everyone to do the same for maximum effect.

The cops just stood there and took all of the hatred with a serious facial expression. They tried their best not to break their poker face, they had to make it seem like getting abandoned by their colleagues from minority communities wasn't a big deal. Even though it was such a messy betrayal that no officer in Deacon Valley P.D. ever expected it to happen. The same way the protesters had no idea that the ball they just catapulted at the officers would make them appear dangerous enough to become nothing more than targets for shooting practice.

12.9 A RACIAL BLOODBATH DECLARED

When the catapult launched and the ball cracked open after it hit the ground, no one expected the plot twist. Even we were gagged to a point of no return while watching it unfold through the lens of the protesters streaming the event. What was expected to come out was a historical compilation of our oppression. From ancestral times until present day, but what actually came out were two dead bodies. They were both White, one was a man wearing a police officer's uniform, and the other a woman wearing an outfit that looked familiar.

Then, a sudden wave of fireworks were launched in the sky, which eventually spelled out the words;

"Suffer In Hell Dylan Maxwell and Norah Matthews!"

When Deandre assaulted us last night, he had to be driving Dylan's car, their dead bodies were probably stuffed in the trunk. And when he got us out of the way, it was the perfect opportunity for him to retrieve the catapult from Deacon Valley High and replace the contents. It was a diabolical masterplan that no one was prepared for, putting everyone at the protest in possible danger.

The Beast Of Liberty truly wanted to get revenge in every sense of the word. For that was the only way to make sure that the officers of the law would get everything that they deserved and then some. He probably brought the catapult to a visible spot, along with the fireworks. Leaving some random fool to do his bidding without being aware of the chaos it would bring as the officers pulled out their beretta's and had a field day.

The entire country was up in arms as it watched a live-stream capturing a modern day massacre at the hands of law enforcement. Everyone watching already knew that there would be hell to pay since all of the streets on this planet would be flooded with protesters hell-bent on seeing justice get served. For what happened here was a barbaric crime against humanity itself.

It was like the officers created a target-based spectrum in their heads based on the shock of seeing Dylan and Nora's mutilated bodies. On the stream it appeared like they were firing at anyone in front of them. But even through the frenzy that turned into a stampede after the first round of shots, we could all see that the only ones not getting caught in this crossfire were White.

The Black and Brown protesters however, were all at risk of becoming collateral damage in this tragedy. It was such a disturbing thing to see it all unfold without being able to do something about it. After all, who do you call when the cops are the ones making us fall?

Even before the shooting had finished, people were already making it go viral, creating the hashtag which would forever be linked to this event, #Blackspeare. As taking in all of these different stories truly resembled a Shakespearian drama told from our perspective. A story of forever trying to find our way in an unjust world that lived to see us all fail, as a way of avoiding seeing us do better than them at every level. Deandre truly managed to create history, and with The Beast Of Liberty still at large, all eyes would be focused on us...

NO JUSTICE
NO PEACE
BLM

OUTRO:

Where Do We
Go Now?

"If you want to go fast,
go alone. If you want
to go far, go together."

African Proverb

THE JUSTICE COLLECTIVE
NO JUSTICE
NO PEACE
BLM
The ultimate Student News
Source to combat the fake
reality of our racist society.

NO JUSTICE
NO PEACE
BLM
THE JUSTICE
COLLECTIVE
We're sorry but this app
was taken down as its
creators are being
reviewed in a federal
police investigation.